RAINBLAST

Mike Willoughby, investigative journalist, was on the threshold of the greatest exposé of his career. He had uncovered evidence that the death in a car crash of the able and hawkish Minister of Defence was not the accident it appeared. Then, suddenly, Mike found himself muzzled—and by the most effective means anyone could have devised. And he was told on the highest authority that the Minister's reasons for purchasing Rainblast, the highly-effective American anti-missile system, were as suspect as his death. Determined to pursue the matter privately, Mike realized that he had to take desperate action when it became clear what really lay behind the purchase of Rainblast.

RAINBLAST

Martin Russell

A Lythway Book

CHIVERS PRESS
BATH

First published 1982
by
William Collins Sons & Co Ltd
This Large Print edition published by
Chivers Press
by arrangement with
William Collins Sons & Co Ltd
1983

ISBN 0 85119 935 6

British Library Cataloguing in Publication Data

Russell, Martin *1934–*
   Rainblast.—Large print ed.
   —(A Lythway book)
   I. Title
   823′.914[F]   PR6068.U86

   ISBN 0–85119–935–6

RAINBLAST

CHAPTER ONE

'Hey, Bob—slow down!'

The young man at the wheel grinned into the mirror. 'Too brisk for you, Charlie?'

'I saw something back there. Just before we hit the bend. Looked like a car on its back.'

'What? Where?'

'Down among the trees. Foot of the embankment.'

One of the girls giggled nervously. 'Probably been there a year.'

Charles Tilhurst gave her a prim look. 'What if everyone said that? Some poor guy might be trapped in the driving seat for two days before someone came along who bothered to look. Can you turn, Bob? I think we ought to go back.'

'Bloody hell.' Robert Bragg looked huntedly around for turning areas. 'We're late as it is. The match starts at three.' He steered for a gateway leading into a field. 'Ella's right—if it is a car, it probably crashed last Christmas.' Crunching into reverse, he backed up and emerged in the direction from which they had come. 'If we're late,' he said despairingly, 'we'll forfeit the match.'

Charles sniffed. 'In that case we'd better not stop. Can't have road casualties interfering with our league position.'

In an uncomfortable silence they drove back to the belt of woodland they had passed a few moments earlier. Robert slowed the car to a crawl. 'See anything?'

'Skid mark,' the other girl said suddenly.

'Where?'

'Across the grass verge.'

'A wheel mark,' corrected Charles. 'Something's ploughed over there.'

Taking the car on to a nearby gravel patch, Robert braked and got out hesitantly. Charles joined him and they stared down the embankment. Robert pointed. 'You can see where it went.'

'Let's get down there.'

The angle of descent caused them to slither, even though the surface was dry. Reaching level ground, they stepped over a flattened thorn hedge into a thicket; two or three birch saplings had been snapped near the base and crushed down into the leaf-mould. A few yards on, among sturdier trees, lay the wreck.

They paused, eyeing it with apprehension. Robert said, 'I think it's an old crash. You can see the rust.'

'Most cars are corroded underneath,' Charles reminded him. 'Let's just take a look inside.'

Reluctantly, Robert stepped closer. 'Nobody in it,' he announced with relief. 'I said it was a waste of time. Come on.'

'You're right,' said Charles. 'There's nobody

inside.'

A note in his voice made Robert look back sharply. Charles had moved round to the other side of the car and was standing motionless, gazing down. Robert's stomach twisted. He made himself follow. The sight was less than he had dreaded, but somewhat more than he had hoped. 'Oh Christ,' he said faintly.

CHAPTER TWO

Mike Willoughby found a note on his desk: *See George*. Dropping it absently into the waste basket, he lifted the phone and asked for a number, loosening his tie while he waited, wondering what had ever become of the air-conditioning that had been promised as part of the trumpeted modernization programme two years previously. A brace of cool summers had disguised until now the fact that the equipment had never been installed: this August, by contrast, was really hotting up, and the newsroom faced south. He scrawled a note of his own on the phone-side pad: *Ventilation?? Speak to Arthur*.

A voice impinged on his left eardrum. 'What have you forgotten now?'

'Just thought I'd let you know, I called in the travel office and the tickets have come through.'

3

'Good. Any surcharge?'

'Fifteen per cent for nine-year-olds as freight. Tell 'em they'll be in the hold with the baggage.'

'You tell them.'

'Willingly. Caroline was the one who wanted to fly that way. How are they both?'

'Not greatly altered,' Lyn said restrainedly, 'since you last saw them at breakfast. They're out somewhere with the Hudson kids. Assuming they show up for lunch, I'll break the good news to them about the holiday. Anything else?'

'George wants to see me.'

'If it's anything big, remind him you're off to Miami in less than two weeks.'

The faint alarm in her voice brought an indulgent grin to this face. 'I think I might slot in an enquiry or two before then. 'Bye now, love. Be good.'

Hanging up, he nodded hello to the *Clarion's* Bizarre Events man, Bill Kemp, who was crawling towards his desk in company with a tangible weekend hangover, and left the room with the stiffened gait of the reluctant part-time gardener. Conscientious though he was about lawn-edges, Mike told himself he had to recognize that the best of his bending days lay behind him. At forty-eight, he tended to find that sinew no longer sprang back into shape with the same readiness as when he was an amateur middleweight who, in his prime, had

4

given an Olympic bronze medallist something to think about over eight rounds of an exhibition match at the National Sporting Club. He smiled reminiscently, though without particular regret. That had been quite a night. Covering the length of the corridor, he stealthily massaged the small of his back, trying to separate bunched muscle in the style of his osteopath and making himself moan softly. Reaching a door, he rapped once with a knuckle and went straight in.

The news editor looked up and indicated a chair. 'Been in a fight?'

'Only with turf.' Mike lowered himself gingerly, landing with a gasp. 'My garden breeds this special grass—green wire. Turns the edge of tempered steel and grows a foot an hour.'

'Move back to an apartment block,' George Pershaw advised unsympathetically. 'Didn't I say the suburbs would be too much for you? Here's something to take your mind off the pain.' He skated two stapled sheets of paper across the desktop. Mike picked them up.

'Godimer mystery,' he read aloud. 'Facts in the case of the late Secretary of State for Defence: compiled by Francis Worth (Crime) and Maurice Trent (Political Staff)...' He glanced up. 'What mystery?'

'Good question.'

Mike sighed. 'You mean, it's the one I'm supposed to answer? I thought it was cut and dried. Godimer left the road while driving himself down to his rural retreat on a Friday night. Dodgy bend, excessive speed ... what's baffling about that?'

'Nothing,' the news editor said mildly. 'Ties in like a dream.'

Frowning, Mike read on. 'What's Trent implying?' he demanded presently. 'So Godimer was heavily committed to rearmament ... so what? Show me three Ministers of the Crown who that doesn't currently apply to.'

'You may be my star investigative reporter,' remarked George Pershaw, 'but you're a lousy grammarian. Any more pertinent comments?'

'Godimer liked to get the best out of a car. Common knowledge. He'd already had a couple of spills. Three years ago he landed a hundred-quid fine for speeding in Constitution Hill. Less than a year ago he piled his Porsche into someone's front garden wall. The guy was a galloping accident.'

'True, as far as it goes.'

'What's more, it appears he'd a drink or two inside him on Friday evening. The equivalent of a couple of Scotches. Nothing lethal, if so, but enough to blunt the reflexes, especially if he was tired after a hard week. NATO discussions, visits to military depots, talks with Service chiefs—the works. Mystery? What mystery?'

'Finish the paper,' murmured the news editor.

Mike scanned it to the end before launching a

slow shaking of the head.

'I'm still not impressed. So he's reported to have been travelling slowly and carefully at a point one mile previous to the bend ... what does that amount to? Unsubstantiated testimony from a none-too-reliable eyewitness who couldn't even be certain he was talking about the right car. And a lot can happen in a mile. From all accounts, that's a temptingly fast stretch of road, slightly downhill the way he was going. He's not the first to have misjudged that bend.'

'Carry on.'

'Before leaving, he'd told his PPS he was going to cruise gently, take his time, so that he could listen on the car radio to the Verdi *Requiem* from that night's Prom. What the hell? Maybe he was lulled into a trance by the music. Or stimulated to recklessness. Nothing conclusive about that.'

'No. But it's one more straw in the breeze.'

'More like a feather in a typhoon. Then we have this question of where he was found lying. On the leaf-mould beside the car, when as a fanatical user of seat-belts he should still have been strapped in—upside down or not. So? He broke his own rule for once. Nobody's perfect.'

'You're not trying too hard, Mike.'

'Wrong, George.' Mike beamed at him. 'I'm trying all I know to dampen your ardour. In ten days' time I'm off to Florida with Lyn and the

7

twins. I'd like to avoid distractions in the meantime.'

'I could fire you for that.'

'Probably.'

'On the other hand, I don't want to. Ten days? Okay: You've got six.'

'Next Sunday?' protested Mike.

'The McMahon probe took you forty-eight hours.'

'Things fell into my lap. In a case like this—'

'So shouldn't you be getting started?'

'Wait a bit. Just what are we aiming to reveal to an astonished readership? An Iron Curtain plot involving their pet Cabinet hawk?'

'It wouldn't be bad for circulation,' Pershaw said musingly.

'Climb off it, George. The choirgirl's revelations about the verger are what sell the paper. Readers aren't interested in how a Cabinet Minister met his end.'

'I'm interested.'

'You're a political nut. You forget, people don't read about politics any more. They read about cults.'

'Where's the difference?'

'And besides, what if we did manage to demonstrate that Godimer's death could have been less than accidental? For the sake of detente, or whatever damn term is in vogue these days, the Government would have to play it down. As for Moscow, they'd blandly ignore the entire thing. We'd be left flapping our arms and screeching. I don't see the benefit.'

The news editor leaned back in his chair. 'I think, Mike, you're arguing against yourself.'

Crossing his legs, Mike threw himself back in turn and investigated the ceiling.

'You're absolutely right,' he admitted. 'How am I doing?'

'Badly. You know the score as well as I do. People generally aren't as cynical and regardless as you're suggesting. A whole bunch of them must have voted for Godimer—or at least what he stood for—last time round. If he was rubbed out by international skulduggery, they're going to want to know about it.'

'And the *Clarion* is set on telling them?'

'Courtesy of Mike Willoughby, arch-dredger ... once he gets his aching limbs off my upholstery and starts behaving like one.' Pershaw switched on the charm. 'As you know, Mike, I've utter confidence in you. Keep me in touch with progress. If it's warranted, we can earmark page one and two or three more inside. Don't worry about pictures. We've shots of Godimer from every conceivable shutter-angle, official, unofficial, semi-official, domestic, recreational, with his family, with his first wife, with his blonde secretary in Junior Ministerial days. Fighting elections, taking parachute jumps...'

'Driving a car?'

'Manipulating everything from a moped to a battle tank. We also have enough prints of the crash spot to stuff an album. They're not good, but if you want to study them, see Tony Welling. He took 'em with a telephoto lens from an upper window of a nearby cottage.'

'Why?'

'Huh?'

'Why did he have to do that?'

'Because,' Pershaw explained patiently, 'of the blanket security. No access to within fifty yards of the scene.'

'What's the position now?'

'I don't know, Mike. Suppose you find out and tell me?'

Mike heaved himelf up, gasping from the effort. 'This is going to cost you. My expenses sheet will gain the fiction award of the year.'

'In a good cause,' the news editor smiled, 'the *Clarion* is all for creative imagination.'

'And if inspiration should fail me?'

The smile lingered. 'Know something, Mike? I've the strangest feeling about this story. I don't believe it's going to fall down on us.'

CHAPTER THREE

As head of the political staff, Maurice Trent cherished a cubicle to himself on the newsroom floor. Here, he brooded long stretches, made careful phone calls, typed memos, arranged lunches with paid informers from Whitehall, and periodically did bending and stretching exercises in the centre of the floor.

He was thus engaged when Mike entered, and with undiminished zeal he kept on, breathing a little hard but betraying few other signs of the effects of more than half a century of studiously-planned existence. Sinking floorwards, he motioned his visitor to a chair and remained for five seconds on his haunches before rising to tiptoe with arms extended horizontally before him, lean fingers stretched, elbows quivering. Slowly he exhaled. Relaxing, he placed both hands on the crown of his head and commenced a series of grinding movements involving his neck-museles. From the side of his mouth he said, 'Don't ... tell me. Let me ... guess.'

Mike waited. With his head listing like the stricken *Titanic*, the political correspondent of the *Clarion* rotated a shoulder as if cranking a rebellious motor, accompanying the action with a rhythmic flexing of the opposite knee. He looked like a puppet with three strings broken

11

out of five. Half-rising, Mike made I'll-come-back gestures and was answered by a switch of physical emphasis from neck to hips. Swivelling energetically, Trent said, 'Don't go. You've seen the report—mine and Worth's? What did you think?'

Mike shrugged. 'That's what I came to ask.'

Trent brought his nerve-centres to a halt. A slight figure in summerweight slacks and a billowing longsleeved shirt, he stood frowning at the floor. Presently he produced a pair of spectacles from a pocket and began polishing them.

'One or two things,' he pronounced, 'aren't right.'

'In your report?'

Trent took gentle offence. 'About the incident. It wants looking into.'

'I thought you and Worth had done that.'

'Sketchily. We were on it over the weekend, but neither of us has the time to give it the necessary attention.' Trent wobbled back to his swivel chair. 'Anything else you need to know?'

'A little about Godimer personally. This country hideout he was heading for—is it really true he was in the habit of spending weekends there entirely alone? I'd heard he used it for total relaxation, but I somehow assumed—'

'It's gospel.' Trent dipped his head several times, like a bird pecking at water. 'You know where the place is, of course?'

'Somewhere near Hawkhurst?'

Taking a comb from a desk drawer, Trent restored symmetry to his cloud-grey wisps of hair. 'Not far from there. Small cottage, two bedrooms, half an acre. He'd had it for years.'

'Family not allowed near?'

'His wife—widow—prefers the ancestral home at Windsor. She hardly ever joined him at weekends. And I know what you're thinking but I don't believe it's true. From what I can make out, he loved the solitude and that's all there was to it. Helped him unwind.'

Mike nodded noncommittally. 'Not even a housekeeper?'

'I dare say someone cleaned up for him, but while he was there he insisted on being alone. Apart from the PM, one or two senior Cabinet colleagues and his PPS, no one had access to him while he was in residence.'

'How long had he owned the place?'

'Fifteen, twenty years. Bought it for a song, had it done up. Apparently he did install a burglar alarm, but that didn't make the security people any happier. Not that there was much they could do about it.'

'But they had a discreet watch kept on the place, presumably?'

Trent peeped at him. 'Your province, Mike, I think.'

'Too kind.' Mike eyed him frostily. 'Let me ask you something more in your line. Did

Godimer, to your knowledge, have more of a taxing period than usual just prior to the accident? Had he been run off his feet?'

'Difficult to answer that,' Trent replied thoughtfully, tensing and relaxing alternate arms as they lay across the desk. 'He always was a glutton for work. Drove himself hard, didn't spare his staff, had this capacity for a sustained—'

'But he was nearing sixty.'

'So?' queried Trent, bristling.

'There comes a time when a man has to concede something to the years.'

'At fifty-seven? Prime of political life. No age at all.'

'Godimer,' said Mike placatingly, 'may well have thrived on work, but was he totally immune from stress? Just lately he'd been heavily involved with the anti-missile uproar, right? To say nothing of the Navy building programme, Rhine Army updating, Service pay ... Then there was the rumpus about cruelty to recruits at training camps. The man was headline fodder for months. Okay, he seemed to be winning his fights—the ones that counted— but you can't tell me there wasn't a cumulative effect on his stamina.'

'If there was,' Trent said obstinately, 'it missed my notice. I lunched with him two weeks ago and he was in tremendous form. He'd just routed his Opposition critics in the House:

14

he'd got the PM and the Treasury to agree big rises for Service personnel ... much against predictions. I'd say his mood when I met him was combative. He looked anything but a tired man to me.'

'People can sag suddenly.'

'Not when they're on top.'

'Getting back to those missiles,' said Mike, after a pause. 'As I understand it, the likelihood now is that the Government will go ahead and try to conclude an agreement with the Yanks for the basing of anti-ballistics on UK soil?'

'Correct.'

'Another snook cocked at the Kremlin?'

'You could say that.'

'Godimer, in fact, seemed to possess the knack of pushing through all the measures least calculated to enchant Moscow.'

Trent gestured neutrally. Thrusting himself clear of the chair, Mike suppressed the urge to release groans while attaining an upright posture: if Trent at fifty-eight could torture himself in silence, a non-smoker ten years his junior had no excuse for audible complaint. 'One final question,' he added. 'Was Godimer having any trouble with his first wife?'

'The whey-faced Rosalind? I wouldn't know about that. She's currently shacked up with some City whizzkid, didn't I read somewhere?' Trent stooped to caress his calves. 'Dulcie will tell you like a shot.'

* * *

A child's voice answered. Mike said cautiously, 'Caroline?'

'No, it's Alison speaking. Is that you, Daddy?'

'Say your name, there's a good girl, after you've given the number. Had a nice morning?'

'All right. We were playing at Mrs Hudson's, only Jimmy tripped and hurt his face so we came home. Do you want Mummy?'

'Just tell her—'

'She's here how.'

Lyn's voice said, 'You'll be late home?'

'Not late: absent. I'm camping at the flat most of the week. Sorry, love.'

'You're on assignment?'

'Some half-witted notion of George's which I'll have to work on, if only to explode it in his teeth. I'll try to get down for the evening on Wednesday. But don't count on it.'

'I stopped counting when I left school.'

'By raising a dust this week,' Mike explained, 'I plan to blind George into imagining that I've done all it's possible to do by Friday. Then I can persuade him to drop the story, and we're clear to take-off.'

'Why, isn't there anything in it?'

'A mass of morbid conjecture. It'll never stand up. Divide a few kisses between the girls,

16

tell 'em they're not to make it tough for you. Got anything planned?'

'I might take them over to Mother's one day. And there's talk of a trip to the safari park with Becky and her pair, if Jimmy's face has stopped bleeding by then. Well, enjoy yourself. Eat properly.'

He hung up, wondering vaguely as always what Lyn considered to be proper in the gastronomic line and deciding yet again that the injunction was not meant to be taken literally. It was her way of saying 'Take care.' He smiled to himself. What did she imagine he got up to on these investigations? Bar-room brawls? Storming of machine-gun posts? Still smiling, he picked up the phone again.

Dulcie was at home and available. He arranged to meet her in Harry's Place at one-thirty. This left him an hour to trace Francis Worth, who was neither in the *Clarion* building nor at his house: a long-suffering wife told Mike he had left at mid-morning to interview someone in connection with revelations about a vice ring in Hackney, and had said he would call at the office later. Mike left messages. Soon after one, the crime reporter put his head around the newsroom door.

'Looking for me, Mike?'

'Yes. Spare a few minutes, Frankie?'

'If it's about Godimer, you bet. You've seen our—'

17

'George showed me. One or two things I'd like to check on.'

'Figured you might.'

'I'm meeting Dulcie at Harry's in half an hour. We can get a head start on her.'

Without discernible reluctance Worth followed him down to the street and across to the *Clarion*'s alternative headquarters, now filling up with bleary-eyed men and women from the dailies. Finding an alcove removed from the hubbub, Mike pressed whisky into his colleague's hand and eyed him severely.

'That thesis of yours gave George big ideas.'

'It was meant to.'

Mike gave him a closer look. He had expected a flippant comeback. 'You're serious? I'd a feeling it was mainly Maurice Trent who—'

'The dossier was a joint one, old boy. Instigated by me, if you want the truth.'

'How come?'

'Conversation with a Very Senior Police Officer. Who in turn was relaying the informal and non-attributable view of a certain high-ranking element of the Force, to the effect that not everything about the Godimer catastrophe was considered to be entirely explicable by the facts as reported.'

'Did he go into detail?'

'Did he hell! When I tried to press him, he curled himself into a ball and rolled away. So, Saturday evening, I went down there

18

and nosed around.'

'And?'

Worth shrugged, spilling a little Scotch. 'You've read the report. A haze here, a discrepancy there. Nothing clutchable. Just this cloudy impression that . . . there's something we haven't been told.'

'You weren't able to inspect the crash spot?'

'The tape must have stretched half a mile. Tony did manage to grab some pictures, long-range stuff . . .'

'Any good?'

'Well, some of them show the car, paws uppermost, in among minced tree-trunks. Beyond that, it could be any other smash scene of the past ten years.'

'What make of car was it, by the way?'

'Jensen Interceptor. Don't you read the newspapers?'

Mike wagged a lazy head. 'Occasionally I write bits of one of them. I understand Godimer was seen by someone—or the car was—driving sedately though a village a mile or so before the crash. Was it you tracked this character down?'

'Not really,' confessed Worth. 'He'd already approached the local paper. It was their stringer, Roger Phelp, who put me on to him. He's the village odd job man, who was just returning home from clipping a hedge on Friday evening when he spotted this Jensen crawling down the High Street, doing about fifteen, he says. Allowing for exaggeration, it does seem that Godimer at that stage was in no hurry—if it was Godimer. It was a warm night, of course. Barnard—that's the hedge-clipper's name—says the car window was open and he could hear choral music blasting from the radio as it meandered past. Well, what he actually said was: "There was these voices, singin' like, with a band an' such." Not the most graphic description of Verdi's *Requiem*, but it does tend to support what Maurice was told by Godimer's PPS.'

'That he intended listening to it on the way down?' Mike nodded pensively. 'How about Godimer himself? Did Barnard identify him at the wheel?'

'He caught a glimpse of *somebody* at the wheel. That's as far as he'll go. I tried to describe Godimer, showed him photos, but I could see he wasn't certain. Apparently it was the car that took his notice. He has a brother in the motor trade, and Barnard seems to have acquired the habit of looking out for offbeat heaps that might interest him. He'll swear to its being Godimer's model.'

'What time was this?'

'Around seven-thirty. Light was still good.'

Mike scowled into his glass. 'Doesn't get us far, does it? A car that could have been Godimer's, seen travelling slowly through a village street on the same evening that Godimer was later found to have crashed. The link's pretty fragile.'

'If you put it like that.'

'What other way is there to put it?'

'You *could* say: Godimer's car was found crashed only a mile from the spot where, that same evening, he was reported to have been seen driving at a leisurely pace through a village, listening to music.'

'Purely a switch of emphasis.'

'But it's helpful to bear it in mind.'

'Only if you're anxious to bend dubious evidence to fit a theory. You wouldn't have some kind of vested interest in this, Frankie? Hopes of a profitable collaboration on the paperback?'

'It would sell a million,' Worth said dreamily. His gaze became fixed.

Dulcie arrived. In addition to a tartan skirt, she was wearing her habitual expression of seraphic docility beneath an outrageous hairstyle that had drawn instant awed attention from the bar at large as she steered a graceful course between tables. Mike rose to greet her. 'Campari?'

'You're after something,' she said composedly. 'Hi, Frankie. How's the muckraking?'

'You should know, my sweet.'

Mike left them swapping insults and went to the bar. When he returned, Worth was leaving.

'Anything more you want, Mike, I'll be at my desk for a couple of hours. Behave yourselves, children.' With a leer in Dulcie's direction he ambled away. She redirected her somewhat overpowering attention to Mike, who from his flanking position was receiving whiffs of a scent evidently concocted by someone with shares in Mothercare. 'He's a funny guy,' she said tolerantly. 'Why did you want to see me, Michael?'

'I'd like to tap your knowledge.'

'You mustn't, it hurts. It'll cost you another drink.'

'Deal. What can you tell me about Patrick Godimer?'

She regarded him contemplatively. 'I've written enough on him, I'd have thought.'

'It's not the column-packing I'm after. I've seen your snippets about his social life. Now give me the goods. What was he really like?'

'That's a frightfully tall order, Michael. I'm Gossip, not Westminster. There's nothing—'

'I'm not asking about his career ambitions. What I want to know is, did he play around? Was there a Good-Time Godimer underneath all that Right-Wing tenacity of purpose?'

'You mean, a really *Bad* Good-Time?' Grudgingly she shook her head, shifting the hairdo alarmingly on its foundations. 'If there was, he hid it terribly well, that's all I can say. Now, if you were to ask me about one or two of his Cabinet colleagues ...' Bringing her coiffure to rest with a shapely hand, Dulcie examined him with a mixture of derision and apology. 'You were hoping for better news?'

Mike gazed unseeingly at the bar. 'I wasn't hoping for anything in particular. What was his relationship with his second wife?'

'They seemed reasonably matey. He had this odd fixation with his country cottage at weekends, but I never heard of any suggestion that he went there for a spot of fun on the side. If he had,' Dulcie added demurely, 'whispers would have filtered through, don't you think?'

'I do think. That first wife of his, Rosalind Carvington—what about her?'

'Fully preoccupied,' Dulcie said decisively. 'She has a thing going with Marcus Hicks, the stores tycoon. No thought for anything else at the moment.'

'She must be fifty.'

Dulcie elevated a beautifully-inscribed eyebrow. 'Is there some kind of legal age-limit?'

'The way I'm feeling,' said Mike, furtively rearranging his limbs, 'there damn well ought to be. In Tessa's case, now . . .'

'She can't be more than thirty-eight.'

'When exactly did she marry Godimer?'

Dulcie pondered. 'I'd need to Consult my Records. I do remember it was just a year after his divorce, which would make it about nine years ago. There wasn't much stir about it at the

23

time, because of course he'd only just entered Parliament: he'd barely been heard of. If it hadn't been for Tessa's connections...'

'His second choice,' Mike observed, 'was an improvement on his first.'

'From a career standpoint, you mean?'

Mike shook his head. 'He was already well in with Langholme—they were buddies from university. And even nine years ago it was obvious Langholme was headed straight for Number Ten. Career-wise, there was no need for Godimer to hitch up with the daughter of a Right-wing Tory peer, however influential.'

'Still, it couldn't have done him any harm. Lord Manninge has a lot of political clout, even yet.'

'I don't say that aspect never entered his reckoning. All I meant was, Tessa's better-looking than Ros.'

'Also, she's a nice person.'

Mike feigned amazement. 'Coming from you, Dulcie, that's quite a testimonial.'

A hurt look strayed into the wide-set blue eyes. 'Gossip-grubber I may be,' she protested, 'but I've not yet become incapable of a balanced judgement. I report what I know.'

Mike patted her hand. 'And what you know of Tessa is mostly on the plus side?'

'Mostly.' The blue eyes met his innocently. 'Don't misunderstand me, Michael. I'm in no position to say categorically that neither of them did any fooling around in their spare moments. What I *am* saying is that if they did, they were both smart enough to keep their activities under wraps.'

'So if it's dirt I'm after, I'm in for a hard time?'

'That rather depends how you go about it. You don't tape conversations, do you, Michael? You jot down old-fashioned notes. Here...' Producing a silver ballpen from a slim vanity bag, she leaned across and slid it into his breast pocket. 'Compliments of the house. My contribution to the investigation. A small thing, but I'd hate to think you were ever impeded for want of ink.'

'Very kind of you, Dulcie,' Mike said, embarrassed. 'I do have one or two of my own.'

'Well, carry it around for luck. If you want to know, I do think you're in for a fairly hard time, but *should* you happen to strike gold...' She turned a sudden guileless smile upon him. '...you won't forget your little professional chum on the fourth floor? She's grateful for any crumbs. And incidentally, she'll have that other drink now.'

CHAPTER FOUR

From the lip of the embankment, Roger Phelp watched the man from the *Clarion* survey the region of the crash spot through binoculars. Spellbound, he waited for comment from the Fleet Street veteran. After two years on a local weekly, Roger was getting itchy feet and he hungered for professional guidance. Sheathing the binoculars, Mike turned and walked back to him.

'Can't make out a bloody thing.'

Roger nodded with quick sympathy. 'It's the best viewpoint there is, but that's saying very little. There's nowhere else you can get even a glimpse of it from the road. Except from directly above, of course, and that's ruled out.'

Mike squinted sourly in the direction of the curve. 'You'd think it was a crashed Cruise missile. How much longer are these barricades going to stay?'

'Your guess is as good as mine.' Roger followed him back to the car. 'At least until the inquest opens, according to my sources.'

'What are they looking for—nuclear radiation?' Mike held the door for him. 'These youngsters who found the wreckage. You've not managed to contact either of them?'

'I called on one,' said Roger, sliding into the

passenger seat. 'He lives in a small town called Butterhurst, six miles from here. Very cagey, he was. Said he'd had strict instructions not to talk about it.'

'His name, again?'

'Bragg—Robert Bragg. He and a friend, Charles Tilhurst, and a couple of girls were on their way to a tennis match at Hastings when they spotted the car. At the time, of course, they'd no idea who the victim was. Having reported the accident, they were apparently made to take a vow of silence. Tilhurst's unobtainable. Gone to ground. The girls are being shielded by their parents. Bragg has at least shown himself, but all he'll come across with is a formal statement . . . probably written out for him. Says nothing.'

Firing the engine, Mike steered slowly down the gradient towards the bend, touching the footbrake as they came abreast of the green canvas screen bordering the verge. The two uniformed constables, one at each end of the barrier, regarded the car inscrutably. Mike gave them both a pleasant smile, inspiring no response. He motored on, allowed the car to gather speed.

'Cheerful pair,' he remarked. 'You'd need a hot-air balloon to see over that lot.'

'One or two of your rivals did charter helicopters.'

'I saw the pictures. Not exactly a howling

27

triumph. A slight excess of foliage 'twixt lens and subject.' Mike twisted his neck to peer back at the road. 'Speaking as a casual motorist with no pretensions to Formula One, I'd rate this curve Easy to Totally Innocuous . . . how about you?'

'At any speed below forty,' Roger agreed.

'Camber reasonable,' Mike murmured. 'Visibility ditto. No humps, obstructions, blind spots. Broad verge, no crash barrier—seems the highway authority saw no need for one. When do they start work?'

Roger grinned. 'Soon as the cops move out.' The grin faded. 'I haven't your experience,' he said respectfully, 'but it strikes me as a heck of a long while for a crash investigation team to be on the job, even allowing for the status of the victim. What would you say? Ever known anything like it before?'

'Several times.'

'Oh.'

'Only difference is, they were jet airliners.'

'Ah.'

'But then again, as you say, he *was* a Cabinet Minister. Could be they're still hunting for State documents.'

'I'd wondered about that.'

The blare of a horn made them jump in their seats. A truck swept past, rocking the car with its slipstream. Mike swerved hastily on to the verge. 'Not the healthiest of parking lots,' he observed, peering around. 'Would that be the cottage?'

'Cottage?'

'One of our photographers managed to grab some shots of the site before the screens went up. He said he took them from a nearby cottage. That's part of a roof, isn't it, above the hillside there?' Crunching the car into gear, Mike glanced at the local reporter. 'Am I taking up too much of your time?'

'Absolutely not. Very instructive, seeing how someone like you operates.'

'Don't get the wrong idea,' Mike advised.'Know what I'm really doing? Proving to my news ed. that this is a phoney trail.'

'You think so?' Roger's face collapsed.

'I'm more convinced of it by the minute. I think Godimer pranged his car and paid the price, and that's all there is to it. Still, for form's sake, here we go. Watch out for a track entrance.'

It appeared around the next bend: a brick-strewn opening in the hawthorn hedge, giving access to a rutted lane that climbed the slope between stake-and-wire fences. On a post a short way up hung a wooden box containing newspapers and a carton of milk: pulling up, Mike removed them and passed them to Roger, who sat nursing the items as the car bounced and lurched to a small plateau at the back of the hill where the lane passed through an open

29

gateway into what could once have been a farmyard but was now a depository for decapitated tree-trunks. Steering between the heaps, Mike drew up outside the front entrance of the cottage. It was built of brick to first-floor level, with weatherboarding above and a topping of tiles into which a dormer window had been introduced at one side. As the car pitched to a standstill they heard a sound like the angry buzzing of a wasp, swollen a million times. Mike cut the engine.

Struggling out, he began hobbling across rough ground towards the porch before, on a change of mind, he turned and headed for the source of the noise. Rounding a corner of the cottage, he came upon a figure wielding a power-saw upon the branches of a felled pine. The bite of the teeth tore at his nerve-ends. Picking his way round to the far side, he faced the user of the instrument, who completed the severance of a timber limb before silencing the motor and looking across enquiringly.

'Something I can do for you?'

Mike introduced himself. 'An associate of mine took pictures from your place on Saturday, I believe.'

'That's right, he did.' The man nodded as if gratified at the memory. He was short but thickly built, with a broad face under a thatch of dark hair, dense eyebrows, large teeth. He wore denim overalls, and was sweating. 'From up there,' he added, gesticulating vaguely at the roof. 'Seemed a bit long-range to me, but he reckoned he could manage. Did he get anything?'

'One or two came out, thanks.' Roger Phelp had wandered into view. Mike beckoned him over. 'We found the milk and papers in your box, by the way, so we brought them up.'

The cottager looked a little startled. 'That's . . . kind of you. Care for some tea?'

'Thanks, we wouldn't say no. Any objection to my taking a quick look down at the road from where our photographer aimed his camera?'

'Help yourself.' The man, who was well spoken, led the way back to the porch, taking the milk carton from Roger before opening the door to a small square hall that smelt of wood-shavings. 'Nasty spill,' he commented, shaking his head. 'I've heard many a squeal of tyres on that bend, but somehow you never expect . . . Then, when it finally happenns, it turns out to involve the best Prime Minister we'll never have. Tragic.'

'You heard nothing of the crash yourself, Mr . . . ?'

'Lucas. No, I was out on Friday evening. If I had, who knows?—I might have been in time to save him.' He pointed, 'If you go up those stairs, turn left at the top and left again, you'll find some rather steep steps leading to the attic. Take as long as you like.'

31

Following instructions, Mike dragged himself wheezily to a bare-floored room with sloped ceilings on three sides, the fourth side consisting entirely of window panes commanding a stretch of the highway near where Godimer's Jensen had spun off into the trees. Part of the canvas barricade was visible, and one statuesque policeman. The shallow angle meant that the woodland immediately below the embankment was now obscured. Hoisting himself on to the sill. Mike gazed through one of the topmost panes, but it made no difference.

In the act of stepping down, he noticed something that lay in a corner of the room. He went and picked it up. After squinting at it on the palm of his hand, he wrapped it carefully inside a leaf from his notepad and placed the tiny bundle in a pocket of his wallet. He turned to survey the room once more before going downstairs.

Lucas was pouring tea from a chipped brown pot into three mugs. 'I was telling your friend, the full weight of the law hit me on Saturday, shortly after your cameraman had left. Questions! Had I noticed any unusual activity around here last week? Did I have any strange callers? Stuff like that.'

'They have to cover everything,' Mike said carelessly.

'Granted.' Their host splashed milk from the carton into the inky depths. 'You're not telling me, though, if that hadn't been the Defence Minister lying dead out there, they'd have gone to all that trouble?'

'I doubt it. Just another road casualty.'

'Well, is there any reason to think it wasn't?'

'None that I know of.'

'What are you sniffing about for, then?' Lucas asked amiably.

Mike smiled. 'Because it was the Defence Minister.'

'Which is why they're still down there, I suppose, poking about in the undergrowth. What in hell are they trying to find?'

'Clues,' suggested Roger, 'to the cause of the crash.'

'I've already told 'em.' Lucas slid a full mug towards each of them. 'That's a deceptive bend down there. People come along fast, think they can make it—then you hear the howl as the treads find they've a little extra to do than expected. Happens all the time.' He consumed half his tea at a gulp. 'Think they'll be wanting me at the inquest?'

'You didn't witness anything. I'd hardly imagine so.' Upending his mug, Mike made signs to Roger. 'Grateful for your time, Mr Lucas. And the refreshment.' Preceding Roger out to the yard, he waited for the cottager to join them. 'Where d'you get your papers delivered from? I'd like a copy of the local weekly.'

'They come from the town,' said Lucas.

'Barnleigh—that's about four miles along the road, going south.'

'Thanks. We'll stop off.'

Lucas gave them a wave as the car lurched off. A few moments later, the giant wasp resumed its complaint behind them.

Roger was silent as they regained the road. Peering both ways, Mike said, 'You're looking broody, old son. Something on your mind?'

'I was just wondering,' replied the local journalist, 'how he gets his papers sent from Barnleigh. We don't even cover that area. Far as I know, all the houses in this district are serviced by Manfield's, the newsagent's in Wadcombe.'

'Interesting,' Mike pulled out on to the highway. 'As for me, I'm asking myself what he'd have used for milk if we hadn't taken it up with us.'

*   *   *

Wadcombe was a village with aspirations towards being a town, but it lacked some essential equipment, such as a focal point. Basically it was a main street with a few stunted offshoots, like a badly stripped fir. Mike, who had first taken Roger Phelp back to his office in Maybank and left him with thanks and a pledge to put in a word for him if he should ever resolve to lay siege to the *Clarion* for a job, had no difficulty in locating Manfield's premises at the corner of a junction: it was the largest shop in the place, and the pavement outside was cluttered with billboards. The young woman behind the news counter proved helpful.

'That's right, we deliver along there. Barnleigh? Oh no—that would be Jackson's, they operate in the other direction entirely. They'd never come out this way.'

'I thought my friend had it wrong,' said Mike. 'Mr Lucas, of Hillbrow Cottage.'

Drawing a ledger towards her, the girl flipped the pages. 'Mr Simon Lucas? Yes, he gets his papers from us. Plus milk every other day and eggs twice a week. We do the lot from here.'

'He can't have been thinking. But then, of course, he hasn't been there long, has he?'

She turned the pages back. 'March ... February ... he's been having deliveries since January, at least.' She beamed sadly. 'He should know us by now. He pays his bill every month.'

'You don't happen to know him by sight?'

'I'm afraid not. We've only dealt with him on the phone. Has Mr Lucas got a complaint, by the way?'

'Certainly not. You give a very efficient service.' Mike stood aside while she sold a copy of *Mother and Child* to a fatigued woman in a smock. 'Speaking of service,' he resumed when she was free. 'I believe there's a gentleman around here who does odd jobs on request. Do you—'

'Alf Barnard,' she said instantly. She glanced at the clock. 'Unless he's working, you'll find him at the Four Compasses along the street. I don't know whether he'll take on anything more at the moment,' she called after him.

Inside the public bar of the Four Compasses, an elderly man wearing baggy flannels and a heavy anorak bulging with zipped pockets was muttering to the licensee over a nearly empty pint tankard. Mike's offer of replenishment, after suitable preliminaries, was accepted with grave courtesy, in keeping with the village handyman's manifest status as a man of dignity, nobody's chattel. Mike handled him with care. Towards the end of the second pint of bitter, by which time they were established at a bench by a window, he eased the conversation around to Godimer.

Alf Barnard's grizzled skull began to oscillate. 'Funny business that. Mighty queer.'

'Uh-huh?' Mike, who was starting to enjoy the sheer incredible rusticity of the performance, kept his tone off-hand. 'Straightforward pile-up, I understood. Enjoyed his motoring, didn't he?' He threw a meaningful wink at the handyman.

Barnard put more energy into his head-shaking. 'Wasn't doin' no speed,' he declared.

Mike regarded him tolerantly. 'How do you know that?'

36

Slowly, the story as told to Francis Worth emerged again, word for word and ungarnished. Under careful encouragement, Barnard showed no inclination to embroider his account. He simply reiterated his conviction that it was Godimer's Jensen he had seen, and that its speed through the village had been no more than twenty. The driver had looked relaxed and was listening to music. If that car had slewed off a bend at high speed a mile later, then Alf Barnard was prepared to swallow his own scythe.

'Fair enough, Alf,' Mike told him. 'But how can you be sure it was the same car?'

'Two Jensens o' that model through 'ere the same evening?' Alf demanded sceptically.

'None too likely, perhaps. But feasible.'

''twas Godimer's car,' Alf insisted. 'I'm not th' only one as says so.'

Mike's fingers tightened about his tankard. 'Oh? Someone else saw him, did they?'

'Pal o'mine.' Alf jerked a thumb. 'Along the road, out o' the village, like. Spoke to 'im this afternoon. He was lookin'.'

'And what did he see?'

'Same as what I did. This here Jensen crawlin' south with its radio on full blast.'

'After it had left the village?'

'Right.'

'But this friend of yours,' Mike said dismissively, 'no doubt isn't so well acquainted

37

with cars as you are. He could have—'

Barnard spluttered into his beer. 'You're jokin'. Runs a repair shop, don't he?'

'Oh. How far outside Wadcombe?'

''Alf a mile. Ask him, he'll tell you I'm right.'

'Does he sell petrol? I'll drop in on him, then. What times does he shut?'

Barnard indicated that the business hours of his friend, David Philcox, were flexible to a fault. In August, he would man the pumps until sundown. Mike said that was a relief, as his tank was running low. He bought Barnard a third pint, discussed the price of agricultural tools and weedkiller, said he planned to visit the parish church and left the pub half an hour later, sauntering with pocketed hands down the main street as though imbued with no desire more urgent than an unhurried assessment of the local architecture. Once out of sight of the Four Compasses, he broke into a trot.

Philcox's Garage (Windscreen Emergency Service, Exhaust Systems While-U-Wait) stood less than half a mile from the village's outer limits. Mike recalled seeing it on his way in. Driving on to the forecourt of shattered concrete, he braked at a pump and got out, stretching himself elaborately and rubbing his eyes. Nobody was rushing to serve him, but he guessed this was rural style and restrained himself from pipping the horn. At the rear of the forecourt was a small office building of blue-painted corrugated iron; to the left, a larger workshop of similar construction stood with its doors open, exposing the crumpled front of a light trunk resting on a jack. PANEL BEATING A SPECIALITY said a sign above the doors.

After a minute, Mike blipped the horn.

Presently he strolled over to the office. The door yielded and he put his head inside. A cash register with its drawer open stood on a table: he could see the ends of pound notes and fivers protruding from a compartment. Nearby crouched a telephone. Two of the walls were occupied by shelves displaying canned aids to trouble-free motoring.

Withdrawing, Mike considered briefly before walking across to the workshop doors.

Beyond the truck, two or three other vehicles in various conditions of bucklement awaited attention. Tools littered the oily floor and a stench of spirit and rubber hung in the air. To the right, an inspection pit took up floor space. He wandered across and looked down. A wheelbrace and a soiled rag lay at the bottom. The only other thing down there was a body.

It lay huddled, its face concealed in a corner. One leg was doubled. For a few seconds Mike stood motionless, looking down. Now that he was making no sound with his feet, an oppressive silence lay over Philcox's Garage.

Presently he left the workshop. Walking to the edge of the road, he surveyed the surroundings. No habitation was in sight. The garage buildings nestled into a steep bank, backed by trees: on the opposite side of the road lay fields, one of them accommodating a herd of cows that were chomping regardlessly on the far side. Returning to the makeshift office, Mike lifted the phone, using his handkerchief, and dialled 999, using a ballpen.

He asked for the police. 'I'm at the Philcox Service Station, south of Wadcombe,' he informed the answering voice. 'There may be nothing wrong, but nobody seems to be around and the till's been left unguarded. Do you think you ought to check?'

'Philcox's,' repeated the voice. 'We'll send someone to take a look. Your name, sir?'

Mike hung up.

CHAPTER FIVE

While driving to Butterhurst he munched a sandwich. On an assignment, Mike always carried a sandwich. He preferred the wrapped takeaway kind, cheese and pickles, encased in the whitest, doughiest bread that scattered the fewest crumbs. Apart from the solitary sandwich and a biscuit or two, he tended to shun food until he wound up for the night. Too much of it clogged his mental channels.

Chewing over the wheel, he wondered whether he ought to have climbed down, examined the body. Made certain.

He knew the question was academic. He had viewed death before.

It felt a little cold-blooded, devouring a sandwich in the wake of such a discovery. But starving himself wouldn't bring Dave Philcox back to existence. Besides, he had given a promise to Lyn.

*　　*　　*

Butterhurst was a town masquerading as a village. Its winding High Street boasted a couple of genuine Tudor structures, a dozen imitations, and some thatch. There was also a market-place, complete with stone water-trough, radiating three minor shopping streets fashioned in nineteenth-century red brick and, here and there, glass and plastics. The place was a development catastrophe.

Mike asked his way to Birch Crescent, part of a raw estate to the west of the town centre. Leaving the car at one end, he walked almost to the other before finding number 83, which also sported a name, Gorse Holme, scratched in Gothic script on an incongruously gnarled hunk of varnished pine attached to the front door. The bell-push produced a double chime. After a delay, the door was tugged back to the limit of

41

its chain. Portions of a face examined him.

'Good evening,' Mike said politely. 'Is Mr Robert Bragg at home?'

'You're Press, aren't you?'

'I am,' he admitted.

'Then I'm sorry, he's not.'

'I may have some information for him.'

The door quivered, failed to close. 'Information about what? He's not able to talk to you, I'm afraid.'

'For his ears only,' Mike said firmly.

The chain scraped off its hook. Seen in its entirety, the face belonged to a woman of about Mike's age: short-haired and bulky, she wore a blouse and slacks and an intense expression behind steel-rimmed glasses. 'Which paper?' she demanded.

'*Clarion.*'

'Not that Sunday gutter-sweeper? Excuse my language. You say you've something to tell my son. You'd better have. I assume it's about the crash?' At Mike's nod she hesitated. 'I'll find out if he wants to see you,' she said finally, and left him standing in the hall.

A multi-hued bird with a hooked bill eyed him from a picture. Mike pulled a face at it. His features were barely straight again when a slim young man appeared from a rear door and approached with clear reluctance.

'You've had a wasted journey, I'm afraid. I've nothing to add to the statement I've already—'

'Understood, Mr Bragg. Is there somewhere we can talk privately?'

'We're using this as the interrogation room,' Robert Bragg said on a note of edgy humour, opening a door to what seemed to be a miniature studio, complete with easel. Tennis gear was piled in a corner. Bragg, who was wearing an open-necked shirt and sneakers, secured the door behind them and apologized for the lack of chairs. 'I gather you've something to tell me?'

Mike dispensed with preamble. 'Regarding the Godimer smash. You might like to know that he almost certainly wasn't speeding when it happened. In fact, all the indications are that he was moving at a dawdle.'

Bragg considered the matter. 'I see.'

'Any comment on that?'

'Should I have?'

'I just wondered whether it might strike you as odd.'

'In what way?'

'That an experienced driver should leave the road at that particular bend when he was doing no speed.'

Bragg mused again. 'I think that's a question for the Coroner.'

'I'd like to know what *you* think. You took that bend yourself.'

'I can hardly put myself in another driver's place. All sorts of explanations are possible. Motoring fatigue. Mechanical failure. I'm

43

talking hypothetically.'

'I did notice that.' Mike smiled. 'What makes you so afraid to speak your mind?'

The young man flushed. 'Afraid? I was told . . .'

He stopped. Mike said encouragingly, 'I guessed you might have been. Who was it—the local police? Or someone from the heavy mob?'

'I've no idea what you're talking about.'

'No, I don't believe you have. You're a little out of your depth. You see, Robert—' Mike injected kindliness into his smile—'you must appreciate, there's more involved here than a routine road accident. It's a matter of public interest, wouldn't you agree?'

'The authorities are handling it.'

'Exactly, and this is where you can help. A security blanket of this kind does nothing for confidence. And it's counter-productive. If I don't investigate, others will . . . and they could play rougher than I do.'

Bragg blinked. 'Everything will come out at the inquest.'

'You believe that? What instructions have you had, so far?'

The young man was silent.

'Believe me,' Mike said weightily, 'you'll end up saying what they want you to say: not a syllable more. It may well be all there is, I'm not saying it isn't. I'm merely offering you the chance to tell me, strictly in confidence, if there's anything else, any single detail that bothers you about what you found last Saturday. Not for publication,' he added swiftly, forestalling an interjection. 'I'm nowhere near ready to leap into print. This is just for my personal file: action pending.'

Bragg eyed him for a moment. 'How do I know you're who you say you are?'

Mike produced his Press card. After a glance, Bragg handed it back. 'Could be forged.'

Mike submitted his driving licence, bank cheque card, badminton club membership document. Bragg returned them all with a shrug.

'If you're a phoney, none of these prove a thing. Still, I'm reasonably positive you're not. The *Clarion* ran a story a few months back, some City corruption exposure, and I remember they printed your picture. You certainly look like the same guy.' He leaned against the easel. 'What exactly is it you want to know? I really can't help much.'

'What you can tell me is precisely what you found, you and your friend, when you first reached the scene.'

He listened while Bragg described the positions of the car and its erstwhile occupant. 'From what you saw of the side of the embankment,' Mike intervened, 'would you say the car had overturned more than once on its way down?'

Bragg frowned. 'I think it's unlikely. I'd say it would have careered straight down before overturning at the bottom.' He tapped the easel with his fingertips. 'To be honest, I don't see any reason why it should have overturned even there. It followed a direct path into the trees. But then, I'm no accident specialist.'

'Okay. Now, as to Godimer himself. Did you get a good look at his injuries?'

The young man flinched. 'I didn't examine him closely,' he confessed. 'I'm a bit squeamish. There was blood on his head. Charlie said he'd probably hit something inside the car before being flung out.'

'Anywhere else?'

'What ... blood?' Bragg shook a doubtful head. 'He was lying face down...' He frowned again, suddenly. 'There was a patch or two on the leaf-mould behind him. I do recall noticing that. It could have been blood.'

Mike considered. 'You both climbed back to the road, and then you drove on to find a call-box? You didn't flag down another car?'

'Nothing came along. It's a quiet road. Used to be busy until they built the motorway the other side of the valley.'

'After you'd called the police, how long was it before they arrived?'

'I suppose about twenty minutes.'

'Did you stick around?'

'We'd no choice. They wanted to ask us

questions. At first they didn't seem that bothered, but then one of them came across and said something like, "Hey, know who we've got here? Only a bloody Cabinet Minister." Then they started to flap.'

'What form did the flapping take, exactly?'

'I heard them putting out radio messages. We were ordered back inside the car and told to wait. After a while, some senior man came along and grilled us for about quarter of an hour. Then he said we could go, but he took our addresses and warned us we might be wanted for further interview later. As we were leaving, a couple more cars came screaming up and formed a sort of cordon around the spot. We didn't see any more. We pushed on to Hastings, but by the time we arrived,' the young man said joylessly, 'the other team had written us off and claimed the match. So we lost the Cup.'

'Too bad,' Mike commiserated. *'C'est la vie.* When was your next contact with the police?'

'That same evening. When I got back from the coast, a pair of plain-clothes men were waiting for me. They asked questions for nearly an hour. Told me not to discuss the accident with anyone—even my parents. Said I'd be besieged by the Press and I was to say nothing beyond what was in the statement they drafted for me.'

Mike rubbed his jaw. 'Did they introduce themselves as police officers?'

Bragg looked startled. 'Not in so many words. I simply assumed ... They said they were investigating the accident and seemed to know all about it.'

'You've not been approached since by the law?'

'No. But I did drop in at the police station this morning, out of curiosity, to ask what had transpired. The duty sergeant just said I'd be notified of the inquest date. That's it, so far.'

'Apart from the Fleet Street avalanche?'

Bragg pulled a wry face. 'I'm not used to such notoriety. Neither is Charlie. In fact, he chickened out ... went straight over to stay with his sister at Hawkhurst before the buzzards could get to him. He even took the precaution of leaving his own car at home—borrowed a friend's Toyota instead. As for the girls, they've both gone to earth. Not that they could tell anybody much.'

Mike took a turn about the room. 'Did you notice a cottage near the accident scene?'

The young man looked blank. 'A cottage? No.'

'There's one half-hidden behind the hill. The upper windows overlook part of the bend.'

'We never saw it.'

'Not surprising. It's a good three hundred yards from the road.'

'What of it?' A thought seemed to occur to Bragg. 'Not the one they mentioned in the papers? The hideout where Godimer—'

'No, he was some way from there.' Mike held out a hand. 'Mr Bragg, you've been most helpful. And don't worry, I won't betray your confidence. What you've told me is non-quotable, for background use only. There's just one other thing ... Where will I find Charlie Tilhurst?'

Bragg's headshake was emphatic. 'Sorry. You'll have to dig him out for yourself.'

*   *   *

There were five Tilhursts in the local directory. At his third enquiry the male voice at the other end of the line said defensively, 'I'm afraid Charles isn't at home. Who's speaking?'

'My name,' said Mike, employing Sussex vowel-sounds, 'is Trevor Dewhurst. I'm match secretary of the High Downs Lawn Tennis and Squash Club at Hastings. Mr Tilhurst's team was due to play us on—'

'Ah, that's right. But they were late, weren't they, and had to concede the match?'

'This is what I wanted to speak to him about. Seems we may have acted a mite hastily. According to the rule-book ... Really I ought to straighten it out with him.'

'I *could* give you a number where he can be contacted,' the voice said dubiously. 'Is it urgent?'

'A little. It's a matter of rearranging the match schedules, you see.'

'Yes, well ... have you got a pen handy?' The voice spelled out some figures. 'You'll probably catch him if you ring now.'

'Sounds like a Hawkhurst number,' said Mike. 'I've a cousin living there. Sandhurst Way. Anywhere near that part?'

'No, the other end—Larch Grove.'

'Very pleasant. Wish sometimes I could move inland, but you know how it is when you're tied down by your job. Well, many thanks indeed. I'll give him a buzz there and we'll see what we can fix up.'

Ringing off, Mike worked his mouth back into shape and returned to his car. The drive to Hawkhurst took twenty minutes, and when he arrived it took him a further ten to track down Larch Grove. Against his hopes, it proved to be a residential road of inordinate length and breadth, containing an assortment of prodigious houses standing in their own grounds, sheltered by deciduous trees and tall fences. His heart sank. Parking the car at an intermediate point, he tossed a mental coin and commenced to his right.

At the first house, nobody answered his ring. At the second, a canine uproar greeted his intrusion, and a leather-faced woman showed a slice of herself for long enough to assure him that she had never heard of a Mr Tilhurst and to request his departure before he excited the dogs. Complying, Mike tried to visualize their behaviour when they really went off their heads, and failed. The occupant of the third house was male and friendlier, but uninformative. He insisted, however, on running through a checklist of the street's inhabitants on his fingers, which lost Mike another four minutes. The next house had three cars parked in the drive, but nobody came to the door.

The fifth house was smaller, a slightly decrepit chalet-bungalow. Almost before Mike had rung, the door was swept back to reveal a middle-aged woman with jet hair and matching eyes, garbed in overalls and grasping a tin of paint with a brush poised across the rim. 'Tilhurst?' she repeated sharply, squeezing excess paint from the bristles into the tin. 'No one of that name around here. After twenty-eight years, I should know.'

'He's staying with his sister,' Mike explained. 'I'm afraid I don't know her married name.'

'Wait a bit.' She put out a paint-smeared hand as though to prevent him running off. 'The Treadwells. They had a strange car in their drive when I came by this afternoon. One of those Jap things.' Condemnation throbbed in her larynx. 'I remember thinking they must have a visitor. The Treadwells would never buy foreign.'

'Which is their place?'

'Third along—Bermuda Villa. You can't miss it.'

The Toyota was tucked beneath a weeping willow at the side of the drive. Striding to the porch, Mike tolled the bell and stood back to inspect the garden vegetation, which was variegated and disorderly. A similar description seemed to apply to the young woman who came to the door. She wore a set of loose-fitting garments, above which threads of tawny hair flowed as capriciously as rivulets on a sandy beach: she looked as if one good pull would divide her into fifty parts. Mike regarded her sternly.

'Mr Charles Tilhurst, please.'

'I think you've come to the wrong house.'

'I think not,' he said courteously.

'There's no Charles Tilhurst living at this—'

'I'm from Department Alpha-Five, Mrs Treadwell. It's imperative that I speak to your brother.'

She narrowed her eyes. 'In that case you'd better come inside.' She made room for him, dusting stray hair away from her face. 'He's watching the cricket. Wait here and I'll fetch him.' Walking away, she added across a shoulder, 'You people never lay off, do you?'

'Have our job to do, madam,' Mike replied agreeably. Tossing the shoulder, she vanished through a doorway. Time elapsed. He studied the prints around the walls of the hall. One of

52

them, depicting a clown explaining a trick to a small boy, was engaging his attention when a stocky man in his mid-twenties appeared. There was an element of truculence in his manner.

'They said I'd be left in peace until the inquest.'

His sister had followed to stand and watch. Mike said curtly, 'One more word, Mr Tilhurst. In confidence, if you don't mind.'

Tilhurst, who was tawny like his sister and wore a droopy moustache which failed to disguise a rather girlish mouth, threw her an appealing glance. She spread her hands. 'Sorr-ee.'

He waited until she had withdrawn. 'I thought you people had done with me yesterday,' he said querulously. 'What more can I tell you?'

Mike lowered his voice. 'It's concerning Mr Godimer's head-wound. You said you examined it fairly closely . . .'

'I said nothing of the kind. I gave it a glance. There was a lot of blood, matted with the hair as you might expect. Who says I examined it closely?' he demanded.

'According to your friend, Mr Bragg, you gave it more of an inspection than he did.'

'I couldn't have given it less. But I'm studying accountancy, you know, not medicine. To me, it was just blood. You've had the experts looking at it, surely?'

53

'We'd still like your opinion. You were the first to find him.'

'My opinion? About what?'

'Whether the injury was consistent with having been sustained in the crash.'

Tilhurst released a snorting laugh. 'How the hell would I know? I'm no pathologist.'

'But you must have drawn some conclusion.'

'I concluded,' Tilhurst said after a pause, 'that I was looking at the latest road accident statistic. What would you have concluded?'

Mike remained serene. 'There's no thought in your mind, then, that the injury could just possibly have occurred a moment *before* the crash?'

This time the silence endured longer. When Tilhurst spoke again, his manner had subtly altered: there was a more moderate note to his voice, coupled with a new caution. 'It's slightly odd you should say that.'

'Why?'

'I'd forgotten till now. My very first impression, as I walked round the car and came upon the body, was that the bloodspots near by...' He hesitated.

'The bloodspots?' Mike prompted.

'They didn't exactly match up to how I thought they should look if they'd been scattered as the body was flung out. There was more of a regular trail to them.'

'As if they'd dripped, rather than been

54

scattered?'

'Possibly . . .' Tilhurst clearly was thinking hard. 'I think the reason it passed out of my mind is that I decided he must have dragged himself a few yards over the leaf-mould before collapsing. I'm not saying I consciously worked it out like that. Up to now I hadn't given it a lot of thought. But since you put the question . . . Does it contradict your own assumptions?' he asked curiously.

'I can't discuss details of the formal investigation. One other point. Were there blood marks on his clothing?'

'Might have been. I really didn't look that closely.'

'You didn't touch the body, lift it at all?'

'I told your colleagues.' Tilhurst looked suspicious. 'Is this some kind of effort to trip me up? I'm not in the habit of fabricating evidence. Why should I? If I'd lifted the body, I'd have said so. But I didn't—neither of us did. Okay?'

'My apologies, Mr Tilhurst. In a case like this, everything has to be gone into and it can get tiresome. You've been very patient and I'd like to thank you for your help.' They shook hands. 'Don't forget,' Mike added severely. 'No contact with Press or television. Don't drop your guard. They'll try to get at you somehow.'

CHAPTER SIX

'Odd question.' The man at the fiction mystery paperback shelf drew a volume carefully, like a tooth from a gum, and scrutinized it as though for bloodstains. 'Why do you ask?'

'Because I'd quite like to know the answer.'

'You? Or the *Clarion?*'

'Same thing.'

'I make the distinction because I know you're apt sometimes to pursue your own hares. But this, I take it, is an authorized assignment.' The man pushed his cushion lips over the flyleaf. His hooded eyes flicked over to Mike and back to the print. He tapped the soft cover. 'Here's what you should be writing, Mike. More your style than exposing things for a news editor. Think about it.'

Taking the book to a cash desk, he paid the girl and received his purchase back in a purple plastic sachet. 'Why don't we snatch a coffee,' he suggested, nodding towards a frond-fringed archway at the further end of the department. 'I've just time. Stuff piling up on my desk. Bits of it may even be of significance. Ever stop to appreciate your luck, Mike, being your own man?'

'Never stop rubbing my hands.' When they were seated at an isolated table, Mike added,

'Ever stop to savour *your* luck, not having to account to a rapacious news desk every four hours?'

'You chose your trade,' the other murmured. 'I chose mine. At least, I think I did. Sometimes I suspect I may have drifted in by accident. Well now, my dear, good morning. You're looking very saucy. Fairly white, please, for my friend. And black for me.' Waiting for the girl to finish pouring, he administered a slap marginally below her lumbar region, earning himself a wriggle of reproof as she moved on. 'One of the few meagre perks left to us,' he remarked. 'This must be the last place in the capital not to have switched to self-service.' Gloom overtook him. 'Any minute now, I suppose.' Brushing his lips with the cup, he winced, put it down. 'You were enquiring about Godimer.'

'So I was.'

'My reply, for what it's worth, is that no portest has yet been transmitted to Moscow, expressing outrage at the indiscriminate spraying of oil on road-surfaces: nor, to the best of my knowledge, do plans of that nature exist. Notwithstanding the usual vague suspicions that may be drifting around, for practical purposes the incident is being played down to approximately point-nought-one on the diplomatic Richter Scale. Sorry, Mike.'

'These suspicions. How vague would they be?'

The hooded eyes pursued the movements of the waitress at the verandah table. 'Godimer,' their owner said abstractedly, 'was by way of being an eagle among hawks. He epitomized what our potential foes might see as the regrettable aim of HM Government to negotiate from strength: by definition, therefore, his departure can scarcely have broken their hearts. On the other hand...' The gaze swung back to Mike. 'Godimer, let's face it, was merely the instrument of Whitehall policy. Nothing much is going to change because he's gone. Forged steel and Mel Beattock may have little in common, but as Godimer's replacement he only has to rubber-stamp Langholme's own strategic decisions. *They're* not going to alter.'

'What if the Kremlin didn't see it that way?'

'Are they so naive?'

Mike stirred forbidden quantities of sugar into his coffee. Even the languid circulation of a spoon brought an ache to his wrist. 'Godimer and Rearmament,' he said thoughtfully. 'The terms were practically synonymous. The Godimer Doctrine. Sure, he had the PM's ear, but what made him appear so truly formidable was the extent of his personal commitment. He was passionate about making Britain strong and he didn't much care who he trampled on to do it. Fair assessment?'

'Close enough.'

'So mightn't it make sense to the KGB to try

putting him out of ciculation, in the hope that his successor would tread more gently?'

'There's no evidence to suggest—'

'What's the medical report on Godimer?'

'That's confidential, Mike. As you well know.'

'Quite right too. What does it say?'

'You'll have me shot at dawn. Pathological findings aren't confirmed, but they strongly indicate what you'd expect from an accident of that sort: consistency with impact against the fascia panel. He was dead before he was thrown out.'

'Bloodstream content?'

'The equivalent of a couple of Scotches. Nothing significant, if he hadn't been exhausted.'

'Who says he was?'

'It's generally accepted. He was never one to spare himself, and he'd had a particularly ferocious week. Three late sittings in the Commons, quite apart from—'

'I've had all this from our political man. He thinks Godimer thrived on the diet.'

'In a way he did. But anyone can get sleepy. Alone at the wheel, quiet road on a warm evening, lulled by music...' The thick lips parted to expose stained teeth. 'I'm not trying to flannel, old boy. If there were the slightest reason to question ... You've excavated nothing yourself, I take it?'

'Nothing conclusive,' Mike said quietly.

The other man waited a moment. 'That's gratitude. I've been frank enough with you.'

'What about those head injuries?'

'What about the bloody head injuries?'

'That's in remarkably poor taste. My point is, it's the sort of description we use in newspapers: it doesn't inform. What part of the head? Crushing or penetration? If the latter, how inflicted?'

'Sorry, Mike. You'll have to excuse me.' The man made preparations to rise. Mike restrained him with a hand.

'Okay: a specific question. Did they find a bullet?'

'Certainly not.'

'You've been told that, for a fact?'

'In my department, people don't go around telling things to other people. A certain amount of intelligent deduction is allowed for. To the best of my—'

'Only it occurred to me,' Mike said lazily, 'that firearms technology must have made giant strides, like everything else, these past few years. Tell me something. Speaking as an expert, would you say that from a range of, say, three hundred yards, it would be relatively easy for a marksman to pick off someone at the wheel of a slow-moving car?'

'From the side? Speaking as an outmoded old fogey, I'd say he'd need all the luck, and then some.'

'But it's possible?'

By now on his feet, the man hesitated. 'Anything's possible.' He seemed to be chewing at a mouthful of eggshell. 'Why from three hundred yards?'

'Why not? I merely offer you the thought, for what it's worth.'

'Thank you, Mike,' the man said after a further cogitative delay. 'I'll probably be in touch.'

*   *   *

Mike was back at his desk, typing out what he had in note form, when his phone bleeped. He snatched it up.

'May I please speak to Mr Willoughby?'

'That's me, go ahead.'

'I'm telephoning on behalf of Lady Tessa Godimer. She'd be willing to see you, Mr Willoughby, if it can be arranged.'

'It's extremely good of her,' said Mike, with a brief prayer of thanksgiving to Dulcie. 'I don't want to intrude at such a time . . .'

'This afternoon is convenient. May we say three o'clock?'

'Fine. Is Lady Tessa at her Windsor home?'

'No, she'll be in Town until the opening of the inquest.' The voice, which was female, young and felicitous, spelled out an address in

61

Knightsbridge. 'We'll expect you then, Mr Willoughby. Thank you so much.'

'Don't give it a thought,' he murmured, after hanging up. He reflected for a moment, then lifted the intercom receiver and tried Dulcie's number. To his faint surprise she was at her post. 'Just had Tessa Godimer's secretary on the line,' he told her. 'I've an audience for this afternoon. Mucha gracias.'

'No trouble, Michael. Glad to be of some help. Listen, can you come up for a moment?'

'Sure.' He typed a line to its conclusion, ran a critical eye down the sheet, ripped it from the machine and stuffed it into a pocket. Although Dulcie's office was only one floor up, he took the lift: his calf-muscles still shouted at punishment. Tomorrow, he promised himself, he would get back to the stairs. No sense in rushing things.

Dulcie was talking languorously into the telephone. Occupying the room's other chair, Mike waited while she ended her dialogue with someone called Shep, or Sep, or possibly Seb, whom she was asking about someone called Heidi, who evidently was rumoured to have broken off with somebody called Alberto or perhaps Alphonso . . . both versions were used impartially by Dulcie between peals of mirth. '*Lovely* to chat with with you, darling. Yes, we simply must get together. No, I shan't. No, just "a friend". Does that make you happier? Then

I'm happy. Bye-ee.' Dropping the receiver, she said, 'Yuk, Tessa's seeing you, then?'

'Thanks to you, I suspect. Your reference must have impressed her.'

'I did lay it on a bit.' Dulcie frowned briefly. 'Something I just wanted to mention to you, Michael.'

'Yes?'

'Between ourselves, it seems there's a possibility that Patrick *was* having a little dabble on the side.'

'Ah.'

'If so, he was very, very discreet. But I learn from an intermittently reliable source that a certain young person not a thousand miles from Whitehall is abnormally desolated at his demise ... golly, how's that for a rounded sonority? I thought you might like to know.'

'Thanks, I undoubtedly might. Did Tessa?'

'Know about it? I wouldn't care to say. Perhaps this afternoon . . .?'

Mike gave her a straight look. 'You're telling me this from disinterested motives, of course.'

'Darling, I do have a column to fill. But if you want to pursue your usual course of being tight-lipped and independent—'

'You'll do a hint-dropping piece anyhow?'

She said demurely, 'What would you do, in my position?'

'I'd clear it with George Pershaw first. He won't be happy if lines start getting crossed.'

Dulcie showed signs of relapsing into a sulk. 'What a rotten trick,' she complained. 'I needn't have even mentioned it to you.'

'No,' he acknowledged. 'But suppose you hadn't, and you'd written your piece. You'd have had space to fill at the last minute when George killed it. I've saved you that.'

'Insufferable man. Flaunting the pen I gave him, and he won't even stretch a point in return.' A smile swam towards her lips. 'What if my tip-off bears fruit, though? Surely that would merit a joint byline on the front-page shriek?'

'Don't tell me you'd want to capitalize on someone else's misfortune?'

'Heaven forbid.' She gazed up at him broodingly, the smile home and dry. 'But I'm a very *concerned* person, Michael. I take a compassionate interest in the frailties of my fellow-creatures. Let me know how you get on.'

Back in the newsroom Mike approached the collapsed spine of Francis Worth, who was puffing cigar smoke across his typewriter and gazing dreamily through the nearest window. 'Frankie, I've come to ask a favour.'

'How goes it, Mike?'

'Do you have a man spare? I'd like him to do something for me this afternoon.'

'What's involved?'

Mike explained. Breathing fumes, Worth said, 'Jimmy Mallard's available. Bright kid.

64

He'll enjoy a country outing.'

'Very grateful,' said Mike. 'I'll be at my flat this evening. Perhaps he could liaise with me there.'

★　　★　　★

The apartment, in a mansion block off Sloane Street, was furnished with some austerity and was clearly a pied-à-terre rather than a residence. A dark-eyed girl in her early twenties greeted Mike in the voice he recognized from their exchange on the phone, and took him through to the main room which overlooked the square. From a couch near the window a tall, slender woman rose and placed her hand in his as though welcoming a constituent to a party rally. 'Could you bring the tea now, Sally?' she asked the girl, past his shoulder.

'Coming up,' the girl said cheerfully. The door clumped behind her.

Unexpectedly, Mike felt awkward. 'It's good of you to see me, Lady Tessa.'

'Not at all. Nice of you to come.' Godimer's widow indicated a cushioned rocking-chair facing the couch. Mike let himself down gingerly. Once installed, he found the motion restful. Returning to the couch, she crossed an elegant leg over the opposite knee and surveyed him gravely. She wore a black skirt and a cream blouse: her hair, copper verging on red, was swept clear of her face into a bundle behind the nape. Good features, thought Mike, with the possible reservation that her teeth were a little large for her mouth. She had fine, penetrating eyes, deep green. Behind it all, no doubt, a shallow brain. He had long ceased to attach significance to outward signs of intellect. Some of the cleverest people he had met had looked like circus clowns. After a short interval she said, 'I'm afraid I don't normally read the *Clarion*.'

'Oddly enough, we tend to be Right-inclined.'

'Which is why you're taking such an interest in my husband's death?'

'We'd be interested anyhow,' he replied, adopting the same candid approach. 'An accident involving a Cabinet Minister . . . one feels it should be accounted for to the fullest extent.'

'Explained, you mean? Is there such a thing as an explanation of an accident?'

He chose his words. 'Sometimes, events can be seen to have conspired.'

Her fingers tapped the arm of the couch. 'You're putting it with great diplomacy, Mr Willoughby.'

Mike's defences collapsed. 'I can put it more bluntly, if you prefer.'

'Let me save you the trouble. Do you have any cause to suppose that my husband's death was other than accidental?'

He looked at her. 'Do you?'

Her voice and expression remained the same. 'I? I'm just the widow, remember. My job ended when I'd identified the body. Why should anyone confide in me after that?'

Instinct told Mike to wait. For a few moments Lady Tessa sat looking out at the square, placid in the mid-afternoon sunlight; she seemed almost to have forgotten him. At the other end of the couch sat a pile of newsprint, a cross-section of Fleet Street, not excluding the *Clarion* whose masthead was visible near the top. Abruptly her gaze returned to him.

'I'm going to go out on a limb with you, Mr Willoughby. When I spoke about not reading the *Clarion* I didn't mean to sound stuffy, though it's true I generally skip a lot of it. However, I do follow Dulcie Mayfield's column—she's an old chum of mine—and when she rang to say you wanted to see me, I asked her about you.'

Mike waited.

'She spoke of you very highly. It seems you can be trusted to respect confidences ... not to leap into print with any old twaddle at the first excuse. I've only her word for that. But I must say, now that we've met, I like the look of you.'

He gave her a solemn inclination of the head.

'Which may sound somewhat arrogant,' she proceed, 'but then I suppose I'm an arrogant

67

person. Which explains why I don't take kindly to being pushed around by tiny tin gods in Whitehall.'

'If there's anything you'd like to tell me...' he suggested.

'Off the record. Is that agreed?'

'I'd prefer it that way.'

'You see, there seems to be a general reluctance on the part of Authority to allow for the possibility—the possibility, let me repeat—that my husband's death was no accident. In the circumstances, I can't regard that as a realistic approach.'

'The circumstances, Lady Tessa?'

Rising, she walked to the window. 'My husband had enemies. Inevitably. He was ultra-Right Wing—at least, in the sense that the people we used to call Left-Wing extremists are now Moderates he was far out on the Right of the party. In more rational times, he might have been known simply as a traditionalist. That alone guaranteed him some flak from certain quarters.'

'Had he received threats?'

She moved an impatient hand. 'The usual cranky letters. Nothing exceptional for a Cabinet Minister. Most of them aren't to be taken seriously. Anyone really wanting my husband out of the way would hardly have broadcast his intentions, do you think?'

'Is there someone you suspect?' Mike asked

bluntly.

Returning to the couch, she sat looking down at her hands for a while.

'As you know,' she said at last, 'there's a strongly pacifist element in the Opposition. For reasons best known to themselves, they don't want this country to have the capacity to defend itself: they'd like it stripped bare. The efforts my husband was making to prevent this must have annoyed them a little.'

Mike couldn't suppress a smile. 'I admire your phraseology,' he remarked. 'Are you suggesting—'

'I'm advancing a basis for enquiry, Mr Willoughby, that's all. Plenty of these Lefties have links with unfriendly Powers. I just think their recent activities should be gone into more thoroughly than seems to be the case. My father takes the same view.'

'Lord Manninge,' Mike said guardedly, 'has considerable influence in Whitehall. Can't he initiate something?'

'Of course he's doing his best. But what you have to realize, Mr Willoughby—as I'm sure you do—is that the British security services can outdo the trade unions in running a closed shop when they choose.'

'You're saying, there may be nothing the Government itself can do? There could be a cover-up?'

'I was called in,' she said deliberately, 'to

identify my husband's body.' A small extra breath left her chest. 'Once that was done and I was over the first shock, I started asking questions. And then, when I was given some very anodyne replies, I began mentioning a thing or two. Just to point them, you know, in a certain direction. And yet somehow... I can't explain it, but they seemed extraordinarily unwilling to be pointed, if you can understand. They would keep insisting there was *no evidence* that the crash wasn't completely accidental.'

'Which isn't your opinion?'

'Mr Willoughby, I knew my husand rather well. If there was one thing he dreaded, it was losing his licence to drive. He'd had two previous accidents: a third one would almost certainly have meant disqualification. Since the second crash, he'd handled a wheel as if it were bone china. Isn't that right, Sally?'

The girl had reappeared, steering a trolley which she introduced deftly into the space between couch and rocker. She nodded.

'Actually, his driving had rather gone to the other extreme—he was agonizingly slow, most of the time.' She turned appealingly to Mike. 'I do hope you can get to the bottom of this, Mr Willoughby. My aunt is right, I'm sure: the crash had nothing to do with speed.'

'We'll see what can be done,' he said cautiously.

'My niece,' said Lady Tessa when the girl had

70

again left the room, 'did a lot for my husband in one way and another. Private typing, that sort of thing. She's almost as devastated as I am.'

'Very attractive girl.' Mike permitted himself a moment's speculation. Susceptible politician; nubile personal assistant recently out of her teens; opportunity unlimited... Catching the discerning eye of his hostess, he abandoned this trail of thought. 'Regarding what you both say,' he added, taking delivery of the teacup she handed him. 'I'm sure it's right as far as it goes, but it's not conclusive. Under stress, people can revert.'

Lady Tessa concentrated on rotating her teaspoon. 'Last Friday evening,' she began, as though rehearsing a statement for the inquest, 'my husband telephoned me at our house in Windsor. He said he was motoring down to his cottage for the weekend, as he often did. He used to paint there, listen to music, generally uncoil. Occasionally he'd work on a speech. I hardly ever went, because I'm not one for rusticating and I knew he valued the solitude.'

The spoon came to rest for a moment. 'Anyhow,' she resumed, 'on Friday he sounded placid, very content with life. He'd had a good week, as you know. Success with Service pay, progress on the anti-missile project ... quite a number of pleasing achievements. I told him to drive carefully, as one does, and he laughed and said, "Don't worry, I'll be crawling. I want to

71

listen to the Prom on the way down." He adored the Verdi *Requiem* and he had this marvellous stereo system in his car, whereas there's only a transistor at the cottage. So you see, he had a positive reason to spin the journey out.'

Balancing the cup on his knees and keeping the rocker still, Mike said, 'I accept all that. But if your husband was so chary of losing his licence, why did he risk drinking before he set out?'

'Who says he did?'

'According to the official report, I understand, there was the equivalent of a couple of whiskies in his bloodstream.'

'Out of the question.' Her tone was decisive. 'He never drank while driving. Barely at all— only if he had to, for social reasons.' Her colour had risen. 'It sounds to me like just one more segment of the overall campaign.'

'Campaign?'

'In support of the accident theory. There's some kind of a conspiracy to convince everyone that he ran off the road.'

Mike gave her a steady look. 'What do *you* think happened, Lady Tessa?'

'I don't know, but how minutely would you say the car itself has been examined?'

'I should guess it's been taken apart.'

'Try asking about it,' she said grimly. 'I have. Was anything found? Nothing, I'm assured. Car in perfect order mechanically, tyres well

72

inflated, no fault in steering or brakes. Apparently, although it overturned, it wasn't that badly damaged. Which is another curious point.'

'How do you mean?'

'If he'd been strapped in, he should have survived. The bodywork wasn't crushed.'

'Presumably he wasn't wearing his seat-belt.'

'He always did. Always.'

Wondering what to do with his cup, Mike finally placed it carefully on the floor, which was carpeted in pale pink. 'Mind if I ask a personal question?'

'I shall probably mind like mad. Let's have it.'

'Was there any ill-feeling between you or your husband and his ex-wife?'

She stared for a moment. 'I can't see what that has to do with it. A certain amount, yes. Ros always resented the break up ... especially when Patrick later made such political strides. But you don't seriously imagine ...? She's associated with a number of men since the divorce, and for the past six months her name has been firmly linked with Marcus Hicks: they're expected to marry. I doubt if she has time at present to dwell upon other things.'

'I'm sure you're right,' said Mike. 'Now, getting back to these other arguments of yours ...'

73

Seeing him out, Lady Tessa's niece held on to his hand. 'Thank you for being so tactful. She's terribly upset, you know, although she puts on a face.'

'I understand that.'

Still retaining his hand, she spoke in a whisper. 'Would it be possible to speak to you in private some time?'

'What's wrong with now?'

She shook her head. 'Not here—it's a bit awkward. This evening? There's a wine bar, Panatto's, just around the corner. Meet me there at eight.'

CHAPTER SEVEN

Closing the outer door of the flat, Mike locked himself into the eye of the hurricane.

Removing his tie, he loosened his shirt collar and stood by the living-room window, gazing down at the burnished tops of vehicles infesting Holborn five floors below, while he debated whether or not to open it. Heat *versus* noise. Aural sensitivity triumphed. Plooding into the bathroom he splashed cold water over his face, groaning from force of habit as he straightened up to grope for a towel.

His head swam a little. He remembered he had eaten nothing really solid for two days. Lyn would have screamed at him. Dabbing at his neck he returned to the living-room and lifted the phone.

'Hi, love. All okay?'

'More or less under control.' Lyn sounded stressed. 'Slight shindig over a stray mongrel the girls found in the park and wanted to keep, but I think I've won. The police have it. How are *you* doing?'

'Fair to middling.' Mike sub-edited any latent zest out of his voice. 'Slow progress.'

'Home tomorrow evening?'

'Do my best. Are they missing me?'

A short pause, punctuated by murmurs. 'I'm instructed to give you love and kisses and please don't forget the books.'

'I remembered to buy them,' he said virtuously. 'They're in my desk. If I don't make it tomorrow I'll deliver at the weekend, without fail. They'll have them in good time for take-off.'

'We can hardly wait,' Lyn said on a livelier note. 'You'll have this job wrapped up by then?'

'No problem.' Mike rapped the telephone-stand with his knuckles and crossed a pair of fingers. 'Now I'm going to fry a couple of eggs. Don't let the terrors give you a bad time.'

'You wouldn't like to tell them that yourself?'

'Tomorrow.' He hung up smiling to alleviate

his guilt-complex. The smallest edge of desperation in Lyn's voice was always enough to cut through to his conscience, strive as he might to remind himself that she had known what she was marrying. They hadn't reckoned on the twins. Luckily, Lyn's widowed mother was a pillar of strength, but she had her own life to lead at times. The school holidays were the difficult periods... God, he reflected uneasily, I'm starting to talk and think like a domestic robot. Shake out of it.

While he was breaking eggs into teacups the telephone rang. The voice that came through was male, youthful, vibrant. 'Mr Willoughby? James Mallard.'

'Who? Oh yes. How did you make out?' Mike had brought a slice of toast in with him, and he went on buttering it as he listened.

'Well, it was tricky. First I rang through from a callbox and the guy answered—that is, somebody did, and when I called him Mr Lucas he didn't contradict me. I passed myself off as an interviewer from the Telephone Users' Association and he co-operated quite amiably, said he was reasonably happy with the service though he'd only been there a few months. I couldn't—'

'Was he well-spoken? Deepish, resonant voice?'

'That's it. After I'd rung off I hunted round for neighbours. Nearest place to his is about half a mile. Farmhouse. I asked the people there if they knew how I could contact Mr Simon Lucas, pretending I'd just called at Hillbrow Cottage and found nobody at home. They were quite surprised, said he was nearly always around, rarely went out. They hadn't been over that way for several weeks, but the last time they saw him he seemed full of bounce and making plans for a kitchen extension, do-it-yourself variety. I said something about him not having the physique for concrete-laying and they said, Oh but he's very well-built . . . one thing led to another and I finally got a fair description out of them.'

'And?'

'The character they know as Lucas sounds much like the guy you met.'

'Oh.'

'But he's something of a mystery man. Took the cottage eight months ago when it was put up for sale by the executors of the previous occupant, some old recluse called Wilson. So far as Lucas has a local reputation at all, he's rumoured to be a writer of some kind. But the population's pretty sparse around there. Apart from this farming couple, name of Hawthorn, the only other place that's anywhere near is the Philcox garage . . .'

'Yes,' Mike said alertly. 'Tell me about Philcox.' Licking butter from his thumb, he chased it down with a bite of toast.

'Well, seems there's nothing to suggest foul play... It only happened last night, by the way. How come you knew about it so soon?'

'Call it genius. It's being treated as accidental, then?'

'Apparently he fell head-first into his inspection pit—chances are he tripped over a wheelbrace that was lying on the floor close by. The till in the office was open, but no cash had been taken. Straightforward misadventure, according to the local cops. Inquest on Friday.'

'Any witness?'

'Nobody saw it happen. It's an out-of-the-way spot, and unless a motorist happened to—'

'Yes,' said Mike, 'I get the picture. Did you manage to talk to Alf Barnard?'

'I went along to Wadcombe, but he was out somewhere on a job and no one could tell me where it was. I tried his home but there was nobody there.'

'You didn't ask at the Four Compasses?'

'I had to get back, Mr Willoughby,' Mallard said humbly. 'Frankie wanted me to—'

'That's okay, I'm not complaining. It's Mike, by the way. You did well and I'm grateful. Thanks for letting me know.'

Deep in thought, he returned to the kitchen and dumped the liberated eggs into the frying-pan. While they were solidifying he remained in a light trance, staring through the four-paned window at the grey-black buildings opposite, seeing nothing but a thirty-foot embankment and a hillside. Roused by a smell of burning and a spitting of fat, he carried the charred remnants of his meal into the other room and, while chewing, watched a quiz show on the television, finding it therapeutic to watch bafflement on other people's faces for a change. The programme was followed by a news bulletin.

Top spot was occupied by the official announcement of Melvin Beattock's appointment as Secretary of State for Defence in succession to the Rt. Hon. Patrick Godimer. The elevation of Mr Beattock, intoned the newscaster, his face vanishing behind a film clip, had surprised some political observers. A former Minister of State for Industry (sequence showing the opening of an electronics factory in the West Midlands), Mr Beattock had later moved to the Foreign and Commonwealth Office (conference scene at Lancaster House) where his chairmanship of the difficult Zembatto Inquiry (handclaps over the draft communiqué) was believed to have captured the notice of the Premier, who in a recent Government reshuffle had given him a junior post in Defence. In this capacity (Whitehall confrontation with top brass) he had consolidated his reputation for grasping what was practicable within a tight budget, and was understood to have helped keep a useful rein on the more flamboyant logistical essays of his late superior.

Meanwhile, continued the newscaster, reappearing, the inquest on Mr Godimer would open the following day and would then be adjourned, pending further enquiries into the precise cause of the crash. It had now been confirmed (film clip of accident spot) that no other vehicle had been involved. One theory receiving attention was that the former Secretary of State had swerved to avoid an animal, possibly a deer, which may have bounded across his . . .

Mike switched off.

Bearing the dishes out to the kitchen he piled them in the sink, ran water over them. Toast crumbs clung to his teeth. Rinsing his mouth, he donned the clean jacket which he kept in the bedroom closet, transferred the ballpens from his other pocket, combed his hair, grimaced at his reflection in the closet mirror and left the flat.

*   *   *

Disappointingly, Lady Tessa's niece looked less stunning under the subdued lighting of a wine bar than she had in the Godimer apartment. From the smart blouse over a flared skirt that she had worn there, she had changed into an unbecoming, square-shouldered suede jerkin over baggy trousers, and her dark hair was severely back behind her ears, much in the style of her aunt. Maybe, Mike thought with a touch of ruefulness, she had opted for leaving him in no doubt that this was a business meeting, nothing else. Not that any other notion had ever entered his mind. It was just nice to feel that a woman had deemed it worthwhile to make a little effort.

A glass of white wine stood already in front of her when he arrived. He asked for the same. Panatto's, he noted, was well suited to confidence-exchanging, being carved into semi-cubicles and pervaded by the sound-swamping hum of air-conditioning. A pricey dive, he guessed.

'Favourite haunt of yours, Miss ... um...?'

'I come here quite a bit. I'm studying the harpsichord at an academy in Brompton Road, and a few of us use this place as a sort of rest-room. Sorry—my name's Sally Channing.'

'Harpsichord. A little dated, isn't it?'

She smiled faintly. 'Ancient music is back in vogue.'

'Are you living with your aunt?'

'No, I share a basement studio with two friends. But I see—I've been seeing quite a lot of my aunt and uncle when they were in Town.'

'Lady Tessa must be glad to have you around at the moment.'

'I think so, yes. It's been a bad time for her.

81

Not just the tragedy itself but all the nasty innuendo. What was he up to, creeping off to the country at weekends while she stayed at Windsor? ... that type of thing. Not easy to cope with when you're feeling stunned.'

'Your aunt strikes me as a fairly resilient person.'

'Oh, she puts a face on. Don't we all?'

Mike eyed her with secret amusement, wondering what she had been called upon to face so far. They took simultaneous sips of wine. Tabling her glass, Sally added, 'She was very fond of him, you know.'

He nodded.

'You don't believe me,' she said accusingly.

'Why shouldn't I?'

'You're thinking, she must have played around a bit. Twenty-year age gap ... left to herself a lot ... That's what you're thinking.'

'Now tell me what I ought to be thinking.'

She drank some more wine. 'Truth of the matter is,' she said on a slight gasp, 'my aunt just isn't that type. Which is the very reason it's never occurred to her that the shoe might have been on the other foot.'

'And was it?'

The girl touched her lips with a paper tissue. 'Of course it was,' she said contemptuously.

'So the weekends weren't just for spiritual recuperation?'

'Oh, the weekends were harmless enough. So

far as I know. I think he really liked to get away. Which is hardly surprising,' she added tartly, 'considering the way he was carrying on while he was in London.'

'Did he play the field?'

'Not Uncle Pat. Deceitful he may have been, but he wasn't stupid. It was this one girl. She works in the Ministry building and she was dotty about him.'

'In my book,' remarked Mike, 'that's noticeably more stupid than spreading the load.'

She looked at him uncertainly for a moment. 'They managed to keep it incredibly quiet. He used to visit her flat about twice a week. Otherwise they kept apart, so hardly a whisper got around. He boxed really clever.'

'Forgive my asking, but how come you know about it, then?'

'Because,' she said, fingering the glass, 'the girl's sister happens to be in my class at the academy and she's kept me informed.'

'Chatty of her,' said Mike. 'Purely in the interests of historical accuracy, I take it?'

'She thought I should know. Then it was up to me to tell my aunt if I saw fit. She was worried about the relationship, naturally.'

'How old is she? The friend of your uncle's, I mean.'

'Twenty-two.'

'Well, if she wanted to get involved with a Cabinet Minister . . .'

'But she's married.'

Mike digested this. 'Did the husband know?'

'Yes. He found out. His work takes him around, but one evening he got back unexpectedly and caught them.' Sally frowned. 'I mustn't give the wrong impression. They weren't actually naked on the bed, so my uncle was able to pretend it was some official business they were finishing off together, and after that, of course, they met somewhere else. But the husband was highly suspicious, though he couldn't prove anything. Apparently he's been going nearly crazy, trying to get his wife first of all to admit it and then break it off.'

'Which she refused to do?'

'Wouldn't even discuss it with him. According to her sister, she's a bit of a young madam who likes her own way, never mind who gets hurt. The husband still dotes on her.'

'So your uncle's death won't exactly have broken his heart?'

'The death of my uncle,' she said with emphasis, 'will have suited him down to the ground.'

Taking a peanut from the dish between them, she chewed it with deliberation, her gaze fixed upon Mike's face.

'This,' he asked presently, 'is what you wanted to tell me?'

'I thought somebody should know.'

'Have you mentioned it to the police?'

84

She shook her head. 'For my aunt's sake, I didn't want it spread around if it could be avoided.'

'Why me, then?'

'You're investigating, aren't you? I heard her say you can be trusted.'

Mike said slowly, 'From the way you speak of your uncle, I get the impression you didn't care for him that much.'

The girl flushed. 'It's my aunt I care about.'

'Then I repeat, why are you telling me this? Wouldn't it be kinder to her to leave things as they are?'

'And let someone possibly get away with murder?' she demanded vehemently. 'That would be unforgiveable.'

Mike sighed and extracted a ballpen. 'Name?' he asked.

CHAPTER EIGHT

At least one TV channel was still flogging the unresponsive hide of the Defence issue when Mike got back to the flat. Switching on idly while he prepared for bed, he found himself watching a semi-formal interview between the Prime Minister and Ivan Partridge, the LBA's resident hatchet-man, who seemed in this instance to be receiving as good as he handed out.

'But would you not agree, Prime Minister, that this represents—or might be *taken* as representing—a not insignificant switch of direction, bearing in mind that Mr Beattock—'

'I've every confidence in Mel Beattock. Let me say—'

'But several aspects of your defence policy—'

'Let me say that had I *not* had confidence in him, I should not have appointed him as successor to Pat Godimer. Furthermore, I've no intention of tying his hands. In due course we shall be presenting to the House . . .'

Mike doused the set, watched the image shrivel. It was almost more than he could do to start undressing. Unutterable fatigue had fallen on him like an oak beam, pinning him in a crouched posture before the screen. By bending a little more, he was able to heave off a shoe and part of a sock before pausing to groan: this time the groan, far from being cosmetic, was forced out of him. Too much wheeled mileage, he informed himself. Too much listening to too many people answering a surfeit of questions. Too little regular exercise. Florida. That was the place to put the process into reverse. Swimming. Tennis. And when he got back, no letting up. Off came the rest of his footwear. Dropping it on the carpet, he walked zombie-like through to the kitchen. Turning on the cold tap, he waited a moment before filling a cup and swallowing a few mouthfuls of water. Using the final gulp to gargle briefly, he choked and had to cough into the sink. Recovering, he stared vacantly through the window at the lights of the traffic below, then leaned to his right to pull down the blind.

Something exploded into his left hand.

★   ★   ★

The pain was inside his head. Pulsations, remorselessly expanding and contracting his skull as if a borehole had been drilled and electric motors inserted, functioning on power surges.

With movement came the groans. At it again, he thought. Now it's agony just to turn over. Irritated with himself, he made another effort and discovered that he wasn't in bed: he was full-length on a floor.

Worse still. Falling asleep before he could reach the sheets. He couldn't recall doing that before.

His left hand and wrist felt clammy.

He raised his head. Instantly the pulsations speeded up, mounted to the frenzy of a trip-hammer as he turned himself to plant both palms on the floor-tiling. Close to where he had been lying, the tiles were slippery. He stared uncomprehendingly at the discolouration.

Thrusting with his right hand, he got himself

to his knees.

Directly below his face, the left hand was a crimson and sticky hash, a bloodied ball of flesh protruding from the shirt-sleeve. Mesmerized by the sight, he fought off a wave of sickness by shaking his head, intensifying the discomfort. It was some while before he could climb shaking to his feet: once upright he stood swaying, hearing the blood-drips make contact with the vinyl. Lifting the hand above shoulder-height, he reeled towards the sink.

Reddened water escaped down the waste-pipe as he held his arm under the cold-water flow. With his right hand he explored cautiously the back of his head, finding a bump that was as tender as a boil. He must have hit the wall when he fell. An insane thing to do. Not content with . . .

He glanced sharply at the window.

The blind was still furled. From the street, traffic noise drifted up to funnel through the circular hole in the centre of what previously had been an intact pane: from the hole, hair cracks radiated outwards like a star-burst. Mike studied it for a second. Then he backed away from the sink, staying alongside the wall-cupboards, making for the door. When he got there, he switched off the light.

Blood and water spattered the carpet as he crossed the living-room to the telephone.

'Emergency. Which service?'

'Ambulance first,' he said. 'Also the police. I've been—'

He stopped. After a moment he replaced the receiver.

Taking another shirt from the closet, he wrapped it about his hand. Clumsily, biting his lip, he dragged both socks one-handed back on to his feet before stepping into his shoes, which were of the elasticated kind. His jacket hung on a chair. Getting it half on, he had to pause again, grit his teeth before impelling the injured hand and its makeshift bandage through the left sleeve: the friction dragged away the protection so that the flesh on emergence was re-exposed. Binding it a second time, he buried it inside the lapel of the jacket and let himself out of the flat.

The all-night clinic was a bare ten minutes' walk from the street door. From the apartment building's rear fire exit, which was the route he chose, the journey time stretched to fifteen minutes because it meant circling the block; and since locomotion at normal pace was more than his head could tolerate, it took twenty. By the time he arrived both shirts had clamped themselves to the gore. Sponging the material away, the Pakistani casualty doctor said critically, 'How did you succeed in doing this?'

'Been practising,' said Mike.

The cocoa-tinted face remained impassive. The last of the fabric peeled off; examining the mess, the doctor wordlessly set about treatment.

An orderly did the binding up. As he was finishing, the doctor returned.

'You must have an anti-tetanus jab.' Mike nodded, reactivating the cranial throb. He winced and hissed. The doctor glanced at him acutely. 'In pain?'

'Just my head. Knocked it when I fell.'

'I'll give you some tablets. Was it a gang?'

'Gang?'

'It's a bullet-wound you have there. You're lucky. It passed through the flesh near the base of your thumb. A little closer to the wrist, you could have bled to death.'

Mike shook his head, very slowly. 'I told you. I tripped against some railings.'

The Pakistani shrugged. The orderly, a silent youth, completed the dressing and went to attend an old woman who had scraped a knee after falling off a bus. Having received his injection, Mike thanked the doctor politely, declined to give name or address and walked out of the clinic, picking his steps like a man treading on soft sand. His legs felt separated, following on one pace behind.

The indirect route back took him nearly half an hour. Regaining the flat, nearly spent, he locked and bolted the door, checked the living-room curtains, sidled into the kitchen and, keeping to one side, with his heart in his mouth, reached for the cord and dragged down the blind. Then he breathed out.

90

He left the light switch alone. Groping his way back to the living-room table, he picked up the reading lamp, found an available socket and used the weak beam to scan the kitchen floor and the rear wall. Almost immediately, at head-height, he found what he had been searching for.

After that, he filled a basin with warm water and set about cleaning up.

★   ★   ★

By the time he reached the *Clarion* building he felt better.

With help from the painkillers he had slept until eight-thirty. Notwithstanding an initial dizziness, it had taken him little more than an hour to wash and dress, and when he reached the sun-beaten pavement he had found it perfectly feasible to walk provided he kept his head stationary on his shoulders. As a precaution, he had brought the doctor's tablets with him.

When he reached his desk he felt wobbly and had to sit for a minute, eyes shut, countering enquiries with a short but colourful description of the railings against which he had stumbled the night before. When the interest and insults had subsided, he buzzed the news editor's office.

'Spare me a moment, George?'

'You got in ahead of me, Mike. Come on up.'

George Pershaw was glancing moodily through some proofs. At Mike's tottering entrance he looked up in evident relief, and eyed the bandaged hand inquisitively. 'Been slugging people around?'

'No, but I won't say the urge hasn't arisen.' Mike fell into a chair. 'Can you stomach a situation report?'

'Sure. What's the reckoning—anybody else on our heels? Everyone's been so fast to swallow the official line, it worries me. Maybe I'm over-anxious.' Pershaw peered hopefully. 'Right now, I get the impression we're out on our own. What do you say?'

'I think you're right. I don't believe anyone else—Press, TV, radio—is seriously questioning the incident. Also, now that Beattock's taken over, attention is going to switch to him. That's the good news.'

'And the less good?'

'I haven't got too far with my own enquiries.'

Pershaw's features took a visible plunge. 'But you've made a start?'

'I'm not sure. The only concrete thing I have to record is that last night someone took a pot-shot at me.'

The news editor jumped in his chair. 'What? Where?'

'At the window of my flat. Telescopic sights and a silencer, I imagine, from across the street.'

92

Pershaw's eyes bulged at the bandage. 'Your hand got in the way?'

'Only because I reached out to draw the blind. I must have moved at the exact instant . . . The shock and the impact threw me back on the floor, so he may have thought he'd got me. I'm hoping so.'

The news editor puffed his cheeks. 'What did the police have to say?'

'I didn't tell them.'

'Mike, you have to. It has to be—'

'Just think. If I make a song and dance about it, not only do we lose the chance of a possible exclusive: we alert the culprits. Everyone's going to be asking why Willoughby's the target. What's the guy up to now? We'd have Fleet Street round our necks. I had to keep quiet.'

'Christ, I'm not wild about this. What if there's another attempt?'

'Obviously I can't rule it out.'

'You're convinced it's to do with this current investigation? Not some hangover grudge arising out of—'

'Again, I can't be sure of that. But if so, it's damn coincidental.'

'I don't want your blood on my conscience, Mike.' Agitation played havoc with Pershaw's vocal delivery. 'You'd best come off the story. It's too big a risk. We've no right to—'

Mike said gently, 'I'm not stopping now.'

'You're nuts.'

93

'Well, I'm mad . . . in the sense of enraged. I tell you this, George. Nothing on earth is now going to prevent me from chasing this up. I don't like violence, especially when it's aimed at me, but it does prove one thing: I've got somebody nervous. That's enough to be going on with.'

'But can you be sure,' Pershaw persisted, 'that somebody was really trying to gun you down? Could have been some young tearaway with an air rifle.'

'No, George. I found the bullet.'

'You did? Where?'

'Embedded in my kitchen wall. It's no airgun slug.'

'The cops should see it,' moaned Pershaw.

'In my estimation,' Mike continued regardlessly, 'the distance between my flat and the buildings opposite is less than fifty yards. No problem for a marksman with the right utensils.'

'If you put the police on to it—'

'They could search the entire block and come up with nothing.'

'Angle of entry of the bullet? They could get a reading from that.'

'Pointless. He's not likely to have left traces.'

'We could put it about that you're dead,' exclaimed Pershaw on a note of inspiration. 'Heart attack. That would take the pressure off.'

Mike chuckled, and clutched his head. 'I

appreciate your concern, but I can't be dead *and* walking around making enquiries. I'll just have to keep my fingers crossed.'

'You won't find that so easy,' the other observed testily, eyeing the bandage. 'Look, Mike, aside from being shot at, do you have anything whatever to work on? Lines to follow?'

'One or two.' Mike explained about Mr Simon Lucas and Hillbrow Cottage. 'If there's a sniper about, I see no reason why he couldn't have been installed in that attic room last Friday evening with a high-powered rifle, ready to take out Godimer as he drove by. Godimer's route to his hideaway must have been known to a few people. Or else easily deducible. Why not?'

Pershaw scratched beneath his collar. 'If so, why no mention of a bullet wound? No hint of foul play?'

'I suppose,' Mike said slowly, 'it's just conceivable that the bullet could have done what it did to me—winged the flesh. Sending him off the road to sustain injuries that disguised the basic cause.'

'Like you, they'd have found the bullet.'

'Not if it passed through the car and out the other side.'

'Hole in the side window.'

'The offside one was down. I've a witness to confirm that.'

Pershaw's head shook feebly. 'Hell of a bit of shooting, Mike. A moving target ... Did you

95

find anything in the attic?'

'Only that one or two of the windows could be opened quite easily. And this.' Extracting his wallet, Mike shook the tiny package on to the desk and, one-handed, unwrapped the paper. Pershaw leaned forward.

'A spent match,' he said blankly.

'Notice anything?'

'Yes. It's a spent match.'

'Not the shape and colour? That's no Western product, George. Observe the rather reddish, grainy effect; also the way the wood is rounded at the end. I was given a courtesy box of just this brand of firelighter when I covered that party congress in Sofia eighteen months ago. It's made in Bulgaria.'

The news editor glanced at him blearily. 'So are my wife's summer sandals.'

'I know we import from Iron Curtain countries. I'm merely placing this alongside what we know about Lucas.'

'What do we know about Lucas?'

'Very little. That's what bothers me.'

Leaning back, Pershaw shaded his eyes. 'If Lucas,' he said presently, 'was a killer, or was housing a killer, would he give someone like you—or a *Clarion* photographer, for that matter—*carte blanche* to nose around in that attic afterwards?'

'If he was smart, that's precisely what he might do.'

The news editor continued sightlessly to ponder. 'Suppose I were to put someone else on this with you?'

'You know that's not the way I operate.'

A weighty sigh came from across the desk. 'In that case, all I can say, Mike, is for God's sake watch out. The obituary column generally shrinks in August. We don't want you expanding it out of season.'

'Stop fretting, George.' Mike stood up. 'When did I ever ask for unnecessary space?'

★　　★　　★

Moments after he had returned to his desk, the telephone bleated. Thinking it was Pershaw with an afterthought, he picked up the intercom, listened vacantly to the silence, realized his mistake and swapped receivers.

'Mike Willoughby? Roger Phelp speaking. Your stringer in—'

'I remember. Good to hear from you again. Have you decided to apply for that job?'

'Not yet. Listen, Mr Willoughby, I thought you should—'

'It's Mike.'

'Sorry, yes. You're still working on the Godimer story?'

'I'm trying not to advertise the fact.'

'Sorry, I forgot. I'll keep this short. You know about Dave Philcox, I believe?'

'Yes, thanks. Got something on it for me?'

'Not on Philcox. It's the other guy, the one who told you he saw the car pottering through Wadcombe...'

'Alf Barnard. What about him?'

'He's dead, too.'

CHAPTER NINE

The Maybank Coroner's Court was housed in a committee room of the Town Hall, a neo-Gothic structure bordering the cobbled square with the permanent vegetable market lapping at its feet. As they were half an hour ahead of the scheduled opening of the Godimer inquest, Mike and Roger Phelp took a stroll between the stalls and breathed in the rich scent of apples. Mike bought a couple of peaches which they ate as they went.

'According to the cops,' said Roger, 'it was the kind of thing that could happen any time to a casual worker. No one actually saw it occur. He was tidying the churchyard yesterday—the one at Wadcombe—and using a powered rotary mower on a grass bank between gravestones. Either he tripped, or the mower bounced off a stone and came back on him.'

Mike winced. 'Where did it catch him?'

'Ankle. Sheared his foot right off. Nobody on

hand to help—he must have bled to death in a matter of seconds.'

'Who found him?'

'The Verger, when he came through the churchyard at about five. Alf had been dead some time. I didn't pick it up till this morning,' Roger added apologetically, 'when I made my calls. I thought it was something you should know about.'

Mike had lost appetite for the peach. He dropped what was left into a litter bin. 'Thanks, you were right. Any more details that emerge, let me know, will you? Inquest date, for a start.'

'Be glad to. Talking of inquests, we'd better go inside and grab our places. Fleet Street's here in strength.'

Returning to the Town Hall entrance, they climbed a mock-marble staircase to Committee Room Two and announced themselves to a harassed Coroner's Officer who, clearly accustomed to handling one Pressman at a time, was badly out of his depth and starting to sink. 'Find seats where you can,' he advised them desperately, and withdrew to mutter over his clipboard.

The extra seating that had been provided was already taken up. Exchanging nods with fellow-journalists, Mike waited while Roger salvaged a pair of folding chairs from the remnants of a stack and added them to the side of a row. 'In the normal way,' the local man remarked gloomily, 'I'd get linage out of this. I hope this lot think it worth their while, travelling this distance for a five-minute hearing.'

'What makes you think they'll spin it out that long?'

The proceedings, in fact, took a minute longer than Roger's estimate. Lady Tessa (*Pale but composed*, Mike saw his neighbour scrawl in his notepad) gave evidence of identification, was thanked and offered sympathy by the small, rat-faced Coroner, and left the court on the arm of her father, Lord Manninge, whose Daimler Mike had seen parked in the square. Although she glanced his way, she gave no sign of recognition. The appearance of the Home Office pathologist created a mild stir, forthwith stilled by the brevity of his testimony. The cause of death, he opined, was head and chest injuries resulting from violent contact with a rigid surface, consistent with the interior of a motor vehicle. The Coroner made notes. The pathologist was replaced by a police superintendent who said that enquiries into the accident were continuing.

'I shall adjourn the inquest for two weeks,' the Coroner said sniffily, and took himself off.

Mike said swiftly to Roger, 'Keep me posted,' and pursued the superintendent from the room.

Drawing level on the stairs, he introduced himself. The wary look in the superintendent's eye became one of active mistrust.

100

'Beyond what I told the Coroner, I'm afraid there's nothing I can tell you. Routine enquiries into the accident are proceeding. We've appealed for witnesses.' He made breakaway movements.

Mike blocked his escape. 'Are there likely to be any?'

The superintendent hesitated. 'Not now,' he said reluctantly.

'So it seems probable the cause of the crash will remain a mystery?'

'It's not for me to speculate on causes. Wait for the resumed inquest.'

'Thank you so much for your help,' Mike said courteously. Watching the superintendent go, he felt a touch on an arm and turned to find himself under scrutiny by a tall, lean, stooped man of about fifty, with shrewd eyes.

'Sorry to butt in,' said the newcomer, 'but I couldn't help overhearing your name and I thought I'd grab the chance of a word. Owen Mitchell. I'm chairman of the late Minister's constituency association. Came along to hear what was said.'

Mike shook the hand that was aimed at his waist. 'I'm afraid you didn't hear much.'

'Shall we talk elsewhere?' With a brisk and yet inoffensive directness, Mitchell steered him downstairs and outside and turned him to the left. 'The George,' he explained, 'is likely to be less populated than the Bull, where there's a rather sensational blonde barmaid who won't have escaped the notice of your colleagues. Done something to your hand?'

'Yes, but I hold a glass with the other one.'

'Good man.' Mitchell fell silent until they arrived at the George's lounge bar, where he laid claim to a table in the corner farthest from the door and, having obtained the drinks, occupied the chair that commanded the broadest view of the surroundings, like a senior officer presiding at a meeting of the escape committee. Beginning to suspect that he had fallen into the clutches of a self-important bore of a party activist, Mike laid plans for an early retreat.

The constituency chairman seemed to read his thoughts. 'I know you're busy and I shan't keep you. The reason I homed in on you, Mr Willoughby, if you want to know, is that Pat Godimer always held you in great respect. There's a man, he used to say, who's not afraid to tread on a few toes if he has to. Never actually met him, did you?'

Mike shook his head. 'He wasn't a great mingler with the Press.'

'In some ways,' Mitchell allowed, 'he was a rather private person. Even the PM—who as you know was a very old associate—even he was a little nonplussed by him at times, I suspect. But then, Pat Godimer was something of a visionary. He saw things very clearly, very broadly, and he had this tendency to lose patience with those who weren't quite as prompt in ... latching on. He liked time to himself, time to think things through. Which is why he used to go down to his cottage so frequently.'

Mike waited attentively.

'From your manner,' Mitchell said with jolting perceptiveness, 'I can see just what you're thinking. Mr Willoughby, please believe me when I say that I'm not here to ladle out the party whitewash, do a paint job on Pat Godimer's moral reputation. It doesn't need one, but that's beside the point. What matters is that it's made crystal clear, right from the start, that he was *not* keeping a French mistress in rural luxury for his weekend convenience.'

'Why is that so important?'

'Because, if there are going to be any hints of a possible security breach, I want them scotched.'

'I'm not aware of any. But apart from that, Mr Mitchell, if you'll forgive me ... how can you be so positive? About his weekends, I mean. Isn't it just possible—'

'That cottage,' Mitchell said warmly, 'was used for rest and contemplation. Nothing else. Great heavens, man, think about it. The place lies on the fringe of a village. A local woman, a Mrs Grant, used to clean it up for him, lay in supplies: she has a key. Now, I don't know how much you know about village life, but let me tell you something: no amount of ingenuity could

103

have kept the arrival and departure of a female secret under those conditions. It's not on. The whisper would have been around in the first week.'

'And there were no whispers?'

'None.'

'With respect, how can you be so sure?'

Mitchell smiled sadly. 'I made it my business to find out. As chairman, I've an obligation to my constituency party to suss out any breath of scandal that might touch our sitting Member. The enquiries I made were discreet but mighty thorough, I can assure you.'

Mike sipped zestlessly at his orange juice. 'Would it shock you, then, to be told that Mr Godimer was having an affair with a young married woman in his own department?'

Mitchell eyed him thoughtfully over his gin and tonic. 'No, because I'd know it wasn't true. You're putting a hypothetical point to me?'

'I'm repeating what I've been informed.'

Mitchell put down his glass with care. 'Tell me.'

Mike outlined his information. Listening intently, Mitchell said nothing until he finished, at which stage he produced a pack of slim cigars, offered it to Mike, who declined, lit one for himself and stretched out on his padded seat, despatching smoke to the ceiling.

'May I see the name?'

Mike handed his note across. Mitchell studied

it for a moment before glancing up. 'Done anything about it yet?'

'I've not had time.'

'It's wrong, you know.' The simplicity of the statement gave it added force. 'Pat would have had to be insane.'

'He wouldn't have been the first. Many a career—'

'We're not talking about human weakness,' Mitchell said impatiently. 'Pat was only mortal, I don't doubt. An eye for a pretty face is one thing. But a girl in his own department? How could he have hoped to get away with that?'

Mike gestured with his good hand. Outriders of a headache were trotting in on him again: finding a painkiller, he slipped it into his mouth and flooded it down with orange juice. Placing a thumb and forefinger against his eyelids, he said, 'When people fall heavily enough, they can cease to care.'

'Pat was a political animal.' Mitchell dropped his voice to a hiss as two men came in and went to the bar. 'On a career level, his instinct for self-preservation was highly developed. Our previous Member, now ... He'd have canoodled with the PM's wife at a State banquet, and damn the consequences. Not Pat. He was different material.'

'Langholme,' murmured Mike, 'hasn't got a wife.'

'No, but he's pretty austere in his outlook.

Doesn't care for any cavorting among his Ministers. If Pat had been reckless to that extent, he'd have been putting his job on the line. And he loved his job.'

Mike ruminated. 'I'm hoping to see this girl later today. Like me to keep you informed?'

'I wish you would.' Mitchell stared sombrely into his glass. 'This niece of Tessa's, Sally Channing ... I've not met her. How did she strike you?'

'Seems a level-headed girl. Perhaps a shade self-righteous.'

'You don't think—'

'She had some kind of a crush on her uncle? The thought did occur to me. But then why would she want to blacken his name—unless it's to get at her aunt, in some twisted way. On the surface, she seems quite attached to her. Besides, if she'd concocted such a story, would she have given me a name?'

Mitchell wagged his head. 'No telling. Thwarted maidens have been known to invent the most fantastic fables and calmly plant them on real people. As a *Clarion* man, you don't need me to tell you that.' He hesitated. 'So far as the accident is concerned, what do you think she was implying?'

'Obviously that it was engineered by a jealous husband.'

'Far-fetched, wouldn't you say?'

'There's an alternative. The husband could

have been blackmailing Mr Godimer, pushing him so hard that the stress became unbearable. In those circumstances...'

'Say it, Mr Willoughby.' Resentment grappled with discomposure in Mitchell's voice. 'Things got so much on top of him that he chose that way of ending his troubles. Is that the suggestion?'

★   ★   ★

Driving out of Maybank, Mike found his thoughts circling like hopeful winged predators about the corpse of Alf Barnard.

A deserted churchyard. No eye-witnesses. How long had Alf been a handyman? Probably most of his life. And using rotary mowers for years. Familiarity could breed carelessness, but for a man who savaged grass for a living to overlook a jutting gravestone...

Mike called on his imagination. It failed to help. To a professional gardener, even a mentally preoccupied one, awareness of danger would have become second nature: auto-pilotage would have taken a hand, as in the case of a motorist ... as it had taken him over now. A signpost told him he was three miles out of Maybank and he had no recollection of covering the distance, although he had been dimly conscious of protests from his left hand as he changed gear at bends. At a time like this, an automatic would have been a help. He'd been thinking about it, in any case, for quite a while. Debating whether or not to make the switch, he put on a little speed: already it was noon, and he had a full programme ahead. He pulled down the sunvisor to cut out some of the glare, which was doing nothing for his headache. Had he sustained mild concussion? Maybe he ought to be resting. On the other hand, the quicker he got back to Town . . .

Topping an uphill gradient, the car began to run away down the other side. He touched the footbrake.

Concussion, he thought, beyond a doubt. By mistake he had stamped on the clutch.

He moved his foot to the right. The engine roared: in a stomach-tossing surge the car leapt forward. Lifting both feet, he experimented with the pedals. Left foot down: engine disengaged. Right foot down: no result. The car went on hurtling between hedgerows, its course erratic: he found himself wrenching futilely at the wheel as if trying to arrest a funfair dodgem car by finding a neutral patch on the overhead pick-up. The sole effect was to bounce the car from one grass verge to the other, with no decrease in impetus.

Furiously he pumped the brake pedal. It flapped uselessly to the floor and back. Clenching his teeth, he hauled on the handbrake.

Pain seared through thumb and wrist. The car faltered slightly, but the gradient was increasing and in a panic of despair he felt it running away with him again, like a hound fixated by a scent. He seized the gearstick.

Before he could attempt a change, a bend loomed. It went to the left on an adverse camber. He braced himself against the seatback.

The strain on his sound arm was terrific. The car hopped to its offside, slipped away from him, headed for a belt of trees. Swerving it back, he felt it rock, heard the screech of rubber and smelt acrid smoke. He was through the bend, but ahead the road fell away in a chisel-straight line to the floor of a valley before ascending at an equivalent angle the other side. He had only to reach the uphill section to coast to a standstill.

At the foot of the descent, a farm track fed in from the right. From its gravelled mouth, a combine harvester was lumbering into the road.

Mike had the feeling he had experienced once before, as a lad on a seaside roller-coaster. He hadn't asked for the ride: a daredevil 'friend' had talked him into it. On the lip of the penultimate swoop, the monster climax of the ride, he had stared appalled into the chasm and had known with a dull certainty that he would not come out alive. And his one thought had been: I needn't have got myself into this. The same phrase drifted through an otherwise empty brain as he watched the combine place two shuddering paws upon the asphalt.

This part of the road had been resurfaced. Almost without guidance the car held a straight course, the wind-noise vying with the engine's howl. The speed now was too great for a gear-change to be contemplated. His bandaged hand remained paralysed on the lever. Both legs stuck out rigidly in front of him, the feet pressed to the floor.

'Pull over,' he moaned.

The hillock of machinery ahead of him was swinging itself about, juddering into line. Its bulk took up two-thirds of the road. From its offside, a metal appendage of vast dimensions dangled into the remaining space, pendulating with the motion.

Beyond the harvester, midway down the opposite hill, another car was approaching at speed.

With a sensation of near-detachment Mike watched it veer to the crown of the road, adopt an overtaking stance. Mechanically he made get-back movements with his head. There wasn't room for one car, never mind two. The attention of the other driver was fixed on the combine: although he couldn't see him (her?) Mike knew this with the same infallibility as he knew that he was about to die, explosively, without an option. God dammit, there was always an option. On a whim, he accelerated.

The combine was changing tack. Its nearside treads found the verge—the dangling metal swung crazily as the contraption tilted. The gap broadened marginally. The other car was fifty yards away. Mike said, 'Oh, bloody hell' and stood on the throttle.

The dancing pendulum whizzed over his head. Instinctively he ducked and then, finding progress unchecked, peered out again and saw the blur of the oncoming car, wrenched at the wheel, shot to the right. The impact, when it came, was from the ground beneath him. The car was bottoming on half-bricks, a belt of them that bordered the road on that side: at the far end, garbage overflowed from a post-mounted waste bin. Further evasive action seemed uncalled for. He sat passive until the structure vanished noisily under the car. For another twenty yards it came along for the ride, heavily entangled with the undercarriage; then, its work done, it escaped with a final metallic yell, leaving the uphill slope and a drainage channel to do the rest.

★   ★   ★

'What's the verdict?'

The mechanic dusted himself down. 'Hydraulic fracture,' he reported. 'Lost all your fluid.' He gave Mike a curious glance. 'Clean cut—like it was done with a knife. You got enemies, squire?'

'Can I hire another car from you?'

The mechanic, an oil-streaked youth with an intelligent face, took the rebuff philosophically. 'Sure. There's a Cortina you can have. How about this one? Take a while to check the damage. Want us to see to it?'

'You might as well.' Mike paid him the tow-in fee. 'Mind if I use your phone?'

'Help yourself.'

Lyn answered wanly. Hearing his voice, she broke into a wail. 'It's being one of those days. The girls were driving me barmy and then the washing-machine flooded the kitchen. I've just finished mopping up and now I've burnt some pastry. I suppose you've rung to say you won't be home tonight, after all?'

Mike counted slowly to three. 'I hope to make it, but I'll probably be late. For unforeseen reasons, I've fallen behind schedule.'

'You'll catch up. Apart from that, how's it going?'

'Fine,' he said. 'One or two small setbacks, but nothing that can't be remedied. The car's gone in for a service, by the way, so I've hired another one for a day or two.'

'All on the *Clarion*, I presume. You've got a cushy number there.'

'Yes,' he agreed. 'Remind me to count my blessings some time.'

CHAPTER TEN

After some delay the door was opened a few inches. Mike positioned himself so that the street lamp shone down on his face. An instant rattling of steel links preceded the full removal of the wooden barrier and its replacement by a grin nestling between hollow cheeks.

'Mikail! It's a thousand years. Anna will be delighted.'

'If I've picked a bad time, Sergei . . .'

'For friends, there are no bad times. Come inside.'

Squeezing through, Mike felt his way up the steep, gloomy staircase, prodded on from behind. 'How is that newspaper of yours? We read it from time to time. We see your name.'

'Then you know roughly how it is. Anna well?'

Joining him at the top of the stairs, Sergei pulled a face. 'She gets bored. Why can't we go out more? she asks me. I say, You go out, I've a book to write. But she says it's no fun by herself. Will you take her for me, Mikail? Give her . . . What's the expression? "Show her a good time."'

'Careful, Sergei. I might take you up on that.'

He followed the other man into a cluttered room. Books and papers were strewn across every available surface. On a table in a corner, an immense manual typewriter with a carriage like the yard-arm of a three-master stood in a sea of stationery and reference volumes: three of the room's battered armchairs were likewise burdened with piles of newsprint and periodicals. Such carpeting as was visible was stained and threadbare. Sergei advanced eagerly towards an inner door.

'Anna! We have a visitor.'

The woman who emerged was as tall as he, big-boned, with coiled hair. At sight of Mike, her broad features lit up: she came forward with arms outstretched, meeting him on level terms. He delivered a smacking kiss to her right cheekbone.

'Annie, you've lost weight.'

'It's because we starve, Mikail. He earns no money'—she jerked a thumb at her beaming husband—'because he does nothing but write, or talk on the telephone. Us, we can live on air. We're better off back in the Ukraine.'

'Anna?'

'He thinks I mean it,' she scoffed, punching Sergei in the ribs. 'And you, Mikail, how are you?' She stood off to inspect him. 'You've hurt your hand.'

'Not me. Someone else.'

'How—'

'Sit down, Mikail.' Sergei swept newspapers off a chair. 'You'll drink coffee with us? Talk

114

about old times. Nobody writes articles about us now ... not since those masterpieces of yours, my friend, that helped us when we first arrived.'

'The book will hoick you out of obscurity, Sergei. How's it coming?'

'Slowly. Slowly. Too many interruptions, you know? Not you, Mikail! I mean the other work, the collation of data. It's good, I like to do it, but when the day has twenty-four hours...' The sunken eyes looked upwards in comic despair.

'So you still have your connections with British Intelligence?'

'Some.' Perching on a chair-arm, Sergei heaved a tumbled lock of hair out of his line of vision. 'Many of the old faces, they're gone, of course. And the new people, they're perhaps more ... cautious? I don't know. Maybe you can't blame them. Whoever heard of Sergei and Anna Poletkov? Who are these funny couple, living in three rooms off Southwark Street?' His laugh was edged with ruefulness. 'When I publish my book... But you didn't come to talk about that, Mikail. You came ... because of your hand?'

Mike held it up gravely, like an exhibit. 'Among other things. Tell me something, Sergei. What are the going methods of KGB execution these days?'

The Ukrainian shrugged. 'They remain versatile. The poison-tip umbrella, the fall from a window, the push under a Tube train...'

'Telescopic rifle too old-hat for consideration?'

'Oh, I would think it still has its place. It must depend on the target, the circumstances. Why do you ask?'

'Someone took a pot at me last night.'

'You're not serious?'

'When I'm still nursing the resultant headache, I have to be. I'll describe what happened: then tell me what you think.'

Sergei listened carefully. 'Do you have the bullet?' he asked. 'Give it here. Yes. Standard NATO issue, Mikail. Used for several years now; well proven.' He handed it back. 'Also extremely painful. You're lucky it was only your hand. Why do you think it might have been the KGB?'

'I'm investigating the Godimer accident.'

'Ah.' Sergei said it on an extended outward breath and looked thoughtfully at his work table.

'Heard anything on the grapevine?'

'A number of conflicting reports, Mikail. Here's Anna with the coffee. Mikail is looking into the Patrick Godimer affair. He was shot last night. At his apartment.'

Handing Mike a brimming mug, Anna made sucking noises and shook her coils. 'You must take care. Don't offer yourself as a target.'

'No, I'm thinking of zigzagging a bit. These

116

conflicting reports, Sergei. What's the consensus?'

'Godimer would have been near the top of the Kremlin's hit-list, of course. They didn't like what he was doing. More power for the British Army, the Naval reforms . . . the missiles. Most of all, the missiles. To be realistic, Mikail, they didn't care for him at all.'

'Would they have thought it worthwhile to get rid of him?'

Inhaling from his mug, Sergei reflected. 'They might.'

'Knowing they'd be obvious suspects?'

Sergei laughed without humour. 'That would worry them, Mikail. That would fill them with stark terror.'

'My thinking entirely. But assuming they were responsible, would they then kill again to cover their tracks?'

'Only for some very special reason.'

'Well, someone's going to a lot of trouble. Yesterday, a bullet through a window: today, another attempt at a car smash. I'm developing a healthy respect for their unhealthy lack of respect.'

He explained about the brake failure. More sucking noises came from Anna. Sergei drank silently to the base of his mug before dumping it on the stiff cover of an atlas.

'It sounds,' he admitted, 'like the work of an organization. It has the smell of the KGB. The shot from across the street ... an agent must have been planted, waiting for you to show yourself. They would have known your London address. It would be easy enough to find out.'

'But that brake pipe must have been severed while I was covering the inquest at Maybank this morning. How would they have known I was going to be there?'

'A logical assumption, perhaps.' Sergei frowned. 'Or a phone-tap ... anything. They have ample resources.'

'That's not all.' Mike told them about Alf Barnard.

'A motor-mower,' Sergei repeated softly. 'Now, Mikail, you are talking. This sounds to me very much like the idea of someone from— shall we say?—east of the Urals.' He turned to his wife. 'You remember Leonid?'

She nodded. 'Could I forget?'

Mike hid his unfinished coffee behind a leg of his armchair. 'On balance, then, you feel this has the hallmark of a Kremlin operation—even though they've loused it up twice, as far as I'm concerned?'

Sergei looked worried. 'I think you must be on your guard. If it's the KGB, they don't miss a third time. Not if they are in earnest.'

'I've been given the distinct impression they might be.' He struggled free of the chair, scattering a bookpile with his left foot. 'Which is why I'm now going to leave you forthwith, before you draw their fire. I'm currently a dangerous guest to have around.' He waved down their protests. 'I've another call to make this evening, anyhow, so I'll be scurrying along, bent double in the shadows. Thanks for your help, Sergei.'

'I've *been* no help.' The Ukrainian looked forlorn. 'Take care, Mikail. How did you come here?'

'By car. But don't worry, it's someone else's. The Cortina I hired is in a lock-up garage in Holborn, relatively safe from intruders with sharpened blades. I'm learning, you see. No harm in taking precautions, even if it does turn out that Godimer's death was accidental and I'm simply having spell of personal bad luck. Good night, Anna. Hammer on at that typewriter. Are you charging him enough?'

'My reward will be a share of the profits.' She gave her husband another poke. 'It should pay for a new jar of coffee. Look after yourself, Mikail. And come and visit us again.'

Sergei saw him out. On the landing, he said, 'You're going back to your apartment tonight?'

'No, I'm going home to Lyn and the kids. But I've spread it around that I'm staying in Town.'

Sergei nodded approval. 'That's wise. I don't believe you're having bad luck, Mikail. I think it's important that you should—what is it?—box clever. Will you accept some advice? Take refuge in numbers. Recruit a team.'

'You sound like my news editor. I can't operate that way, Sergei. You know I'm a loner.'

'Everyone knows,' the exile said significantly.

Returning to the car, Mike wondered briefly whether Sergei's counsel was sound. To a limited extent he had followed it already, but his concession fell some way short of the team effort that both the Ukrainian and George Pershaw had urged, and in a silent South London street after sundown the force of their arguments seemed suddenly to have been multiplied by a factor of ten. Angry with himself, he decided to sleep on the thought, knowing that by morning his outlook would be safely back to normal. In the meantime, he was not above quickening his pace a little and pursuing an erratic course along the footway. No one had ever called him pigheaded.

Parked next to the blank wall of a house, the Renault hatchback of young Jimmy Mallard looked lonesome in the shadows. The junior reporter was sitting at the wheel. Entering by the nearside door, Mike said, 'Hope I wasn't too long. They're very hospitable. Over to Fulham now, if you don't mind.'

Mallard said nothing. He seemed loath to make a move. Mike threw him a glance. 'Forgotten something?'

Then, more sharply, 'James?'

He touched the other's shoulder. Mallard

120

swayed, toppled against the offside door.

Mike wrenched at the nearside handle. Before he could open the door, Mallard slowly regained an upright position and palmed his eyes. Drowsily he muttered, 'I could sleep for a week.'

Restocking with breath, Mike sheepishly removed his fingers from the handle. 'D'you make a habit of that?'

With a self-conscious grin Mallard tweaked the engine into life. 'It's less habit,' he said, pulling away, 'than biological make-up. When I'm tired, I slip into a trance. I lost a job that way, once. My boss thought he'd met a case of dumb insolence. Where in Fulham?'

Mike gave him the address and turned to look through the rear window. A van was following them. He kept a check on it until it turned off, to be replaced by a white or cream saloon which presently yielded to a forty-seater coach. Then he relaxed. Mallard's driving was dashing but adequate, and it was a relief not to have to use his left hand. He sat back with closed eyes, trying to ignore the subdued warning tick inside his head.

The Fulham street they wanted was part of a one-way system. Negotiating the maze, Mallard found an unlikely space between abandoned vehicles and occupied it adroitly. 'Ninety-three,' he read out, craning his neck. 'Fifty-eight shouldn't be more than a hundred yards along.'

'Go back to sleep,' Mike advised, crawling out. 'I may be a little longer this time.'

★   ★   ★

The house had been converted into flats, like most of the others in the Edwardian terrace that ran the length of the street. The middle of the three bell-pushes beside the street door was labelled JOHN AND CYNTHIA HOSKIN. Mike pressed and waited. An entryphone coughed at his elbow.

'Who is it, please?'

'Mike Willoughby, *Sunday Clarion*. I'd like to—'

'Just a moment.'

A slim-built young woman with a pleasant, open face came to the door. 'I've been half-expecting the Press,' she said, studying him intently. 'Would you like to come up?'

She had not asked for proof of identity. Possibly she recognized him from the mug-shot that sometimes accompanied his column: it was only twelve years out of date. He followed her into a high-ceilinged yet stuffy room, tastefully decorated and furnished, heavily carpeted. A TV set was tuned in muted shades to the latest episode of *Philadelphia*, the most recent junk import from the States. With a decisive movement she doused the picture.

122

'Do sit down. I can offer you sherry or . . .'

'Nothing for me, thanks.'

'My husband's out at the moment.' Seated straight-backed on a basket-chair arranged at an angle to his, she folded her hands on her lap and looked down at them before glancing up again. 'I think I can guess what you've come about.'

Rarely had Mike been eased so painlessly into an interview. He was almost at a loss. The aura given off by Cynthia Hoskin was one of wholesome directness; he felt a compulsion to be equally forthright in return, but instinct and training held him back. He gained a little time by resettling himself and crossing his legs.

'According to some enquiries I've been making—'

'It's Patrick, isn't it?'

He gestured acknowledgement. Her eyes flickered towards his bandaged hand and returned to her own neat thighs. 'I knew,' she said, low-voiced, 'it would have to come out.'

'Do you feel able to tell me anything about it, Mrs Hoskin?'

'What is it you'd like to know, exactly?'

'Perhaps,' he suggested, 'we might start with some background. How long have you been working for the Defence Department?'

'Two years.'

'In a secretarial capacity?'

'That's right.'

'And when did you first come into personal

123

contact with Mr Godimer?'

'A year ago. Eleven months, to be accurate. His private secretary was off sick and they wanted someone with a good typing speed to do some urgent work for him. I was called into his office and that's when we met.'

'How soon did you form a relationship?'

'It took a little while,' she said, with a hint of primness. 'I was only there three days, the first time. Then the secretary returned and I went back to the pool. A couple of weeks later we happened to meet in the corridor...'

'You and the Minister?'

'Yes. He remembered me and asked how I was getting on. I said, to be polite, I said I'd preferred working directly with him, and he laughed and said something about having to see what could be arranged. A day or two later, to my surprise, I was called in again.'

'To deputize for the secretary?'

'Supposedly. But I honestly didn't do much. While I was there, though, he asked if I was ever available for overtime. I told him I was married but that my husband often worked late or was away on business, so I probably could put in extra hours from time to time. He just nodded, and I thought no more about it until the following month—last October.'

'What happened then?'

'He called me in and asked if I was available for a rush job. My husband was in Manchester that week, so I said I was. He told me to report to his office after working hours and to bring some files. He gave me a signed chit for the ones he wanted. But when I took them in, he didn't seem that interested. We drank coffee together and he started asking me about myself, how I liked it at the department, did I regard him as a slave-driver . . . things like that. He was terribly nice. We seemed to hit it off. You know, there was just something between us.'

She gave a small hiccup and stopping talking. Mike gave her a few moments. 'Did matters develop at all that evening?'

Taking a quick breath, she brushed her face with the back of a slender hand. 'It got to the point where he was telling me about his own . . . domestic shortcomings.'

'Specifically?'

'Oh . . . How he drove himself hard because there wasn't a lot to go home for. His wife had her own circle and they saw very little of each other. She hardly ever came into London. He didn't say it unkindly—he wasn't that sort of a man. It was more a case of reading between the lines.'

'And how did you react?'

'I think I said the usual things. How hard it was to combine home life with a career, how people had to be tolerant and how things sometimes gradually improved. It was then that he looked at me, very straight, and said,

125

"They've improved already."'

'What was your reply to that?'

'I couldn't think of anything to say. Not that there was any need, because from that moment we had an understanding. Things just took off.'

'When did the friendship become intimate?'

'Two nights later. He asked me in for more overtime, and when the building was quiet he put out the light and locked the door and we ... we made love on the window-seat.' Her gaze returned serenely to Mike's. 'I felt no guilt whatever. Perhaps I should have done, but I didn't. He was so gentle. As a lover he was very considerate, not at all ruthless as you might have expected, and when I—'

'How often did you meet, after that?'

'Two or three nights a week. He made me feel a complete woman, for the first time. I'd thought I was in love with my husband, but Patrick ... He made me realize just what I'd been missing. Although, as I say, he was kind and gentle, he was incredibly passionate. I remember once, during working hours, he suddenly dragged me into a sort of deep cupboard that opened off his office—'

'Can I take it, Mrs Hoskin, you're willing that we should print some of what you've told me?'

She regarded him steadily, her posture unaltered. 'It's bound to leak out, isn't it? I'd rather the full, correct story was known from the start. I don't want distorted versions. It was

126

too good a thing for that.'

Mike scribbled briefly in the notepad he was nursing. 'Did you ever go to his Knightsbridge apartment?'

'No. We agreed it was too risky.'

'So where did you meet, apart from his office?'

'Here.'

'Wasn't that even chancier?'

She shook her head. 'No one takes much notice of anyone else in this district. As long as he took precautions, like wearing dark glasses and a hat with a brim, there was no problem.'

'But what about your husband?'

'As I said, he's away a lot.'

'I understand, though, he did arrive home unexpectedly one evening.'

Rising, the girl took a controlled turn about the room, arms clasped across her breasts. 'That's perfectly true,' she said quietly. 'Patrick and I had already made love—on that sofa there—and got dressed again, but my husband's no fool. He could see how things were. He didn't shout or rave. He just warned Patrick, in so many words, that unless it stopped he'd tell the world what was going on.'

'In view of that, did you end it?'

She stopped in her tracks to stare down at the carpet. 'Of course not,' she said softly. 'How could we?'

'Did your husband *think* you'd ended it?'

'He's too astute for that.'

'Was the subject referred to again?'

'Oh yes—continually. John kept threatening to expose the relationship.'

'What held him back? He'd nothing to lose, surely?'

'Me,' she said simply.

'You'd have walked out on him?'

'He knew that if he'd ruined Patrick, he'd have seen the last of me.'

'You made this clear to Mr Godimer?'

'Yes, but of course he didn't know John as I do. He took the threats more seriously. Kept saying we'd have to stop seeing one another. We even agreed to, once or twice. But each time he came back. He couldn't help himself.'

Mike jotted another note, a short one. 'There's one point, Mrs Hoskin, I'd like clarified. When you and Mr Godimer were meeting in his office, did it never strike you as extraordinary that a man in his position would take such fearful chances? Couldn't he have managed something more discreet?'

'I think he found it exciting. A test of his ingenuity. He liked a challenge. Besides, there was quite a romantic atmosphere to his office, you know. You could see the river from the windows. It was almost like a honeymoon hotel room.'

'I see. One other thing. Do you happen to recall whether you saw each other during the week of July nineteenth to the twenty-sixth? That's a couple of weeks before his death.'

She nodded without hesitation. 'We were never apart longer than two or three days. I remember that week clearly. He came here twice.' Opening a shoulder-bag that stood on a dresser, she extracted a tissue and blew her nose.

Mike stood up, pocketing the notepad. 'Thank you, Mrs Hoskin. You've been most forthcoming. I don't think I need intrude any more on your privacy.'

She gazed at him, liquid-eyed. 'You're sure you have everything you want?'

'I've all I need.' On his way to the door, he paused and turned. 'But if I might offer a word of advice, Mrs Hoskin, there's something I think *you* could find helpful.'

'What's that?'

'In future, check your facts. Patrick Godimer wasn't in London during the week from the nineteenth. He was in Brussels, attending a NATO conference. If he'd flown back for a couple of assignations, I hardly think his absence would have gone unnoticed.'

'Just what are you suggesting?'

'I'm suggesting you seek psychiatric help. It might prevent you wasting other people's valuable time.'

Her face contorted. 'Get out!' she screamed. 'Get away from here, you sodding bastard, do

129

you hear? Bugger off!'

★   ★   ★

Mallard was awake. As Mike fell into the car he touched the ignition key and waited for orders. The pair of them sat motionless for a while until Mallard lost patience.

'Somewhere else?'

Mike emerged from reverie. 'Yes. Back home.'

'The Surrey hills?'

'No, I wouldn't do that to you. If you can drop me off at Holborn I can collect my hired car. Thanks for your help tonight.'

'No sweat.' Diplomatically, Mallard forebore to ask why his senior colleague couldn't have driven himself around, bandage or no bandage. Taking the car out of the one-way maze, he headed east. 'Get anything out of her?'

'Wasn't necessary. She was only too keen to deliver.'

'Good story?'

'Sensation.'

'Wow.'

'One trifling reservation. She made up the entire damn thing.'

'She *what*?'

'Female fantasy. She's living in a world of her own. Took me a while to catch on: when I did, I'm afraid my reaction was a bit ham-fisted. I could have let her down lightly, but I didn't.'

Mallard whistled sympathetically. 'Understandable. Leading you up a blind alley . . . She never had it off with Godimer?'

'I doubt if they even met. Husband's walked out on her, is my guess, leaving her to work on her mental embroidery. Devil of it is, she's plausible. Fooled her sister, it seems, with her fairytale, and one or two others besides. I should have known. But it had to be checked.'

'Sure. So, it's back to square one?'

Mike slumped against the backrest. 'Not quite, I hope.'

*　　*　　*

Lyn was in bed, reading a woman's weekly in the pinkish light of the bedside lamp. Mike went over and kissed the top of her hair. It had a coarse, crackling texture against his face. Her nightgown sagged at the straps, giving him an uninterrupted view of one plump breast and part of its twin. She looked up from the page with a toothsome smile.

'What's that in aid of?' he said suspiciously.

She thumped the magazine with a thumb. 'Do your utmost, it says here, to give a welcome to your old man when he staggers in from work. Remember, one glimpse of a sour expression can be the last straw that broke the camel's hump. Thought I'd give it a try.'

131

He sat on the bed. 'Write and tell 'em it doesn't work.'

Now that he was seated on the edge of a sprung mattress with a rug under his stockinged feet, he felt incapable of further movement. He stared numbly at his dim reflection in the dressing-table mirror. Putting aside the magazine, Lyn eyed him searchingly.

'Been overdoing it?'

'Nope.'

'I'd hate to see you when you had. Anything of interest this evening?'

'I met a young woman in her apartment.'

'I hope she gave you every satisfaction.'

'She gave me a headache. Sorry, love. I'm drained. I just want to crash out.'

Lyn said sharply, 'What did you do to your hand?'

He looked at it vaguely. 'Gashed it on a railing. It's all right.'

'Were you drunk?'

'Probably.'

'Let's have a look.'

'There's nothing to see.' Drawing away, he rose unsteadily, fumbling with his necktie as he made for the other bed.

'Come here.' Climbing out of the sheets, she planted herself in front of him and began tackling the knot. 'What with a headache, a gashed hand and a drained circuit, you're a bundle of comfort and no mistake. Were you really seeing a woman?'

'In the line of duty.'

'But naturally. Good-looking?'

'An eyeful,' Mike said tonelessly. 'And if you want to know, she succeeded in turning me off human relationships more effectively than a sex manual in the space of about twenty minutes.'

Liberating the tie, Lyn loosened his collar and moved closer. 'Maybe you could do with some reversion therapy, then.' She slipped a strap of the nightgown.

'Sorry, Lyn. I'm just not in the mood, okay?'

'Come and lie down anyway. After a little while you'll start to feel more relaxed, and then—'

'For Pete's sake! Can't you lay off for one evening?'

She stepped back, replacing the strap. 'I didn't realize you felt that way about it. Pardon me for intruding.'

He tried to pour warmth into his voice, knowing the damage was done. 'You look terrific, love, and I'm a miserable swine. I apologize. I didn't mean to snarl.'

'Perhaps you should go back to your lady-friend, whoever she is.' Lyn was returning to bed. 'She seems to do a better job.'

'Now that's stupid. She's a head-case who—'

The lamp went out. The sudden blackness obliterated his words more effectively than an explosion. He stood chewing his lip, thrashing a lifeless brain for placatory noises. His hand as well as his head was beginning to throb. Finding another painkiller, he smacked it into his mouth and continued painfully to undress, doing his best to be soundless but unable to avoid creating a bedlam of creaks and rustling that filled the bedroom as though animated by some need of their own to poison the air.

Before turning back the coverlet he paused again, listened for the sound of Lyn's breathing. It was shallow but regular. Too regular. A number of feeble contenders for conciliation jostled for position on his tongue, all to be put to rout as he toppled to a horizontal position and lay oscillating gently, ears alerted for possible overtures.

None came. With an inward moan, coupled with a generalized curse upon fantasizing females, he turned on to his side.

CHAPTER ELEVEN

'Am I speaking to Mike Willoughby?'

The voice, like the eyes, possessed a hooded quality, as if tailored for partial coverage of otherwise nude areas. Even from a telephone earpiece it was unmistakable. Mike said, 'This is quite an honour. Usually it's me calling you.'

'Don't let it give you ideas above your station.

As a general rule, Pressmen still rate low in our order of priorities. It's merely that, in view of the fact that you were trying to help, I felt I owed you the outcome of my enquiries. The reply to what we were discussing is negative.'

'What we were discussing...' Mike heaved his mind back. 'The bullet, you're talking about?'

'Would you mind keeping your terminology on an inexact level? I'm sure your recollection of what we were talking about is as clear as mine. The answer is, there wasn't one.'

'Or, if there was, it's not being referred to?'

'The reply is negative, Mike. That's all I can say.'

He stared across the newsroom, seeing nothing. 'How about the injuries? Does the report—'

'Nothing of significance beyond what I mentioned. All right, old boy? Must go now.'

'Thanks for wasting time on me,' Mike said sardonically.

Dropping the receiver, he sat comatose for a moment until a couple of Weird Occurrences reporters wandered in and tried to get him involved in some pre-noon horseplay. 'Sorry, boys,' he excused himself. 'Pressing business to attend to in the Morgue.'

* * *

In addition to the more recent clippings that had yet to be processed, there was a wealth of information on film and tape. Barry Craddock, the chief records clerk, showed him how to work the projector. 'Don't often find you down here, Mr Willoughby,' he observed with humour. 'Thought you carried your own filing system around.'

'There are times, Barry,' Mike told him, 'when mind has to yield to the machine. Did you dig out the stuff I mentioned?'

'I think you'll find it all there. Take your time, Mr Willoughby.'

Apart from laying everything on for him, Barry had gone to the length of screening off a corner of the Morgue to provide a makeshift browsing cubicle. Settling himself at the metal desk, he started with the cuttings.

Most of them concerned events that he could readily recall: only a glance was needed to ginger his memory. In nine weeks, which was approximately the period covered by the cuttings, Godimer seemed to have done enough to fill the average man's lifetime. The impression, Mike knew, was slightly illusory. Any leading politician's documentary record would have suggested the same. Allowing for this, however, the diversity of the late Minister's activities in the months preceding his death was an eye-opener. When he had not been presenting Defence White Papers to the House or rising to repulse verbal assaults at Question Time, he had been visiting the Rhine Army by helicopter or rumbling across Salisbury Plain in a tank turret. In less frenetic moments, he had not been remiss in attending NATO meetings, being briefed by Service chiefs, and having fruitful discussions with counterparts from the Third World. On one occasion he had been seen with his wife at the opera.

Except for a close study of Lady Tessa's expression in the accompanying photograph, Mike wasted little time on this material. Turning to the tapes, he selected some of the earliest and fed them to the magazine.

The newspaper and magazine reports they preserved went back to Godimer's university days. As a member, along with Ralph Langholme and at least three other members of the present Government, of the renowned Coverdale Set, he had been earmarked even then for likely political advancement. A former specialist college, Coverdale had achieved university status during the 'thirties, although it was not until after the war that it gained its place in the front rank of ideological breeding-grounds from which the Right Wing renaissance had eventually sprung. There were pictures of Godimer as a round-faced twenty-year-old in the early 'forties, earnestly in debate with others of the Coverdale Set, among them Langholme and the present Home Secretary, Henry Puttenham.

The same names, attached to faces which had thinned out and lost hair in the intervening years, cropped up in later photographs. Langholme and Godimer at a Party Conference during the 'sixties, leading the rebellion against the 'watery radicalism' of the current leadership: the pair of them, in a famous incident, ostentatiously turning their backs upon the rostrum, declining to applaud the Leader's concluding speech. They had dared and won. Knocked out of his stride, the hapless Leader had talked openly of dropping them from his Shadow Cabinet; but he had left it too late.

By the early 'seventies, with their positions consolidated, they had turned the tables. Ralph Langholme took over the party reins. Godimer, Puttenham and others of a like philosophy such as Nigel Mainwaring, Far-Right product of a comprehensive school designed to avert just such a disaster, marched in close attendance. The dawn of a new day was at hand.

Barry Craddock poked his head around the screen. 'Find what you were looking for, Mr Willoughby?'

'Not yet, Barry. But I'm certain it's here somewhere.'

There was film of Godimer's adoption as a prospective Parliamentary candidate, plus considerable footage of his storming election campaign in which he was abetted by his first wife, the formidable Rosalind, daughter of Sir Horace Carvington, a former Ambassador to Washington. She was shown wearing silly hats and kissing babies. Godimer's sensational victory in a marginal had been followed almost instantly by his appointment to a junior post in the Foreign and Commonwealth Office, in which capacity his handling of the Krakovic Incident had passed into legend.

Coming shortly before this, his divorce and subsequent remarriage had attracted no more than routine attention. Most of the publicity there was had been inspired by the involvement of Lady Tessa, a society pet of the period. It was not to be long, however, before the emphasis shifted. Godimer's meteoric progress through a series of appointments marked him as a man to watch, and the media began duly to log his every movement.

Watching the filmed record, Mike leaned forward abruptly.

Reversing the projector, he re-ran a sequence, froze it at a certain point and left his chair for a closer look. The scene depicted had been shot some years previously at a party rally. It showed a group of Left-wing demonstrators breaching a security cordon and hurling smoke-bombs at the Prime Minister and his associates, Godimer included, inside the foyer of the convention hall in Liverpool. Langholme had an arm up to protect his eyes, while Puttenham and one or two others were gesticulating to someone out of the picture; but it was to the extreme left of the frame that Mike's attention was directed. After a minute's scrutiny he turned and stepped out of the cubicle.

'Barry,' he called.

The records clerk glanced up from a wall-cabinet and hurried across. 'Mechanical trouble, Mr Willoughby?'

'No, it's working fine. I'd just like your opinion on something.'

Gratified, Craddock followed him inside. 'Take a look at that,' Mike invited. 'Ignore the central figures. Concentrate on the one just inside the picture on the left—the one in the beret, chucking something. Can that be who I think it is?'

Peering myopically, Craddock exchanged his glasses for another pair. He nodded.

'That's her all right,' he agreed. 'Who'd have thought it? Never knew she even took an interest in politics.'

*　　*　　*

The man standing at the bar made an analytical study of his whisky glass from several viewpoints before committing part of the contents to his throat. From a smooth, circular face, eyes of an apparently childlike candour

140

switched course to rest upon Mike's bandaged hand. He retracted it. The gaze climbed to his hairline.

'I'm not trying to flannel you, old boy. We've heard nothing.'

'Does that mean there *is* nothing?'

'Can't be definite about that. I'm not on the memo-list of this one.'

'So it's big?'

The other gave him a kindly smile. 'Or possibly rather small.'

'Is that your opinion?' Mike asked after a moment, 'or more in the nature of a wild surmise?'

With a glance along the bar, his companion cupped his mouth with a hand. 'Special Branch officers aren't paid to make guesses. Tell you what, Mike. I'll lay what I know on the line. The car's been gone over with phase-contrast microscopes: no sign of tampering. All the damage resulted from the crash. Godimer ditto. He wasn't force-fed a rare poison, or dope. Okay, he was a Cabinet Minister, hence he rated more than the customary five lines in the local *Express and Herald*. That's all there is to it.'

'Not quite all,' said Mike.

'Huh?'

'There's also the curious affair of the two eye-witnesses.'

'What eye-witnesses?'

Mike offered details about Philcox and

141

Barnard. The Special Branch man listened tolerantly.

'You're assuming rather a lot, old boy. Hardly witnesses, were they, in the accepted sense? As for their deaths, that has to be down to coincidence. Anything else is the purest speculation.'

'Newspaper investigators,' said Mike, 'aren't paid not to speculate.'

'Come to that, it needn't be so coincidental. The two of them were buddies, you say. So, Philcox kills himself by falling into his own inspection-pit. Barnard, shocked and upset, drifts into morbid reflections while cutting the grass and fails to notice the edge of a gravestone. Entirely logical sequence of events.'

'It can be made to sound like it.'

'In any case, their evidence wouldn't have amounted to a row of beans. Neither of them saw the crash.'

'You're saying that evidence of driver-behaviour before an accident is inadmissible?'

'Of course not. I'm merely trying to keep things in proportion.'

'So am I.'

'You're not succeeding too well. Listen, Mike.' Solemnity encroached upon the guileless eyes. 'You've never let me down yet, so allow me to repay in kind. My honest opinion is, by continuing to chase this angle you're liable to make something of a fool of yourself. That, I should hate to see. What happened to your hand?'

'I think someone was trying to make something of a corpse of me.'

The Special Branch man gave him a doubtful look. 'You mean, your wife was after your blood? Maybe she agrees with me. Maybe she considers this latest crusade of yours is a non-starter and feels inclined to damage your typing fingers. I wouldn't blame her. I tell you frankly, Mike: if you're planning some kind of vaguely insinuative splash in this Sunday's edition, I believe you'll be displaying less than your normal standard of judgement.'

'Thanks for the warning,' said Mike. 'At least I'm trying to bring judgement to bear, which is more than I can say for some.'

*   *   *

The Commons debate, ten months previously, had been notable more for emotion than force of argument. The outcome had been predictable. Where the defence of the realm was concerned, a Government Back-bench rebellion against Cabinet decisions was unthinkable. By a sizeable majority, Godimer had duly received the go-ahead to open negotiations with Washington for the purchase and installation of a complete Rainblast anti-missile system to shield the British Isles by the mid-'nineties.

The cost, according to a follow-up article by the Defence Correspondent of the *Custodian*, was theoretically to be shared. In practice, the brunt would fall upon the purchaser, although it would be offset to some degree by a handful of minor weapons contracts. Despite being acclaimed by the Premier and his hawks, the deal was still viewed with disquiet by some experts. They feared increasing dependence upon US technology, leading ultimately to a 'buy or die' situation in the arms market.

Godimer and his team refuted this. Rainblast, they pointed out, was an operational reality, whereas any comparable British system would take up to a decade and a half to develop. More crucially, it was years ahead of anything yet available to Moscow. In the assessment of Whitehall, it was a bargain not to be missed.

The remainder of the article touched on the technicalities of the system. Mike skim-read it before returning the back-number with thanks to Maurice Trent, who was carrying out calf-stretching exercises with the aid of his desk and a footstool, grunting between contortions and purple in the face.

'You won't be happy,' Mike observed, 'till you've killed yourself and hung your body out to bleach. That's helpful, Maurice. Thanks for hunting it up. Any idea what stage the negotiations have reached?'

'On Rainblast?' Trent suspended convulsions

to wheeze for a moment. 'I imagine they're well advanced. Assuming, of course, there's no change of tack now Godimer's gone.'

'Is that likely?'

'Not unless Langholme's picked the wrong man. Which I can't think is conceivable. He's too keen to finalize the deal. He knows Godimer had the confidence of the Yanks, so he'd be anxious to replace him with somebody equally acceptable. So far, Mel Beattock seems to be making all the right noises.'

Trent commenced work on the other calf. Mike watched him, humming tunelessly. 'Know anything about Beattock?'

'How d'you mean?'

'For instance, was he one of the Coverdale Set? He doesn't seem to figure much in our records.'

Trent applied self-massage. 'I think you'll find he was a year or so after the others, but he did have connections. Politically, he's been something of a dark horse till now.'

'Did he support the Right-wing revolt in the 'sixties?'

'In a quiet way.'

'Hedging his bets?'

'Just doggedly loyal to Langholme, I'd say. Which no doubt accounts for his latest appointment. Some people are saying that Langholme, in effect, has taken over Defence himself.'

Mike said thoughtfully, 'Maybe he felt he had to.'

*   *   *

'The front?' George Pershaw repeated. An expression of beatitude began to wrestle with the contours of harassment crowding his face. 'You can have the entire damn issue if you need it. Are things looking good?'

'Another day or two and I'll let you know.'

'Give us a break, Mike. What have you come up with?'

'Willoughby's Assorted, with tough centres. Mind if I hand you the finished box, tied up in ribbon?'

'So long as the ribbon's a good, loud scarlet.' Dropping his felt-tip marker, the news editor leaned back luxuriously. 'Not even a hint?' he said hopefully.

'Sooner not, George. I could be wildly at sea.'

'Oh, great. So Friday afternoon you saunter in to mention that the story's fallen apart and would I mind remaking the paper while you start again. In any case, what about supporting items? Pictures, background, recaps . . .'

'You can prepare all that. Whatever happens, I'll have something for you, even if it's largely a kite-flying exercise. I'm hoping it'll be something less nebulous.'

'*You're* hoping?'

'One other thing. I'll be working from home

146

for the rest of the week. The kids like to set eyes on me occasionally and I've got my peace to make with Lyn.'

'Ah. Trouble?'

'She wasn't talking when I left this morning, and the fault was mine. I'd like a chance to patch things up.'

'Best of luck, fellah. When can I expect the copy?'

'Noon on Friday, at the latest.' Mike paused at the door. 'Could be something quite big, George.'

Pershaw released a hollow groan. 'What's your middle name, Tantalus? Get out.'

Upstairs, Dulcie was typing languidly in a cloud of mentholated smoke. From the open doorway Mike said, 'You might like to know, Pat Godimer comes through with a clean bill of matrimonial health so far. Sorry.'

Returning from afar, she rewarded him with an exquisite row of teeth. 'Sweet of you, darling. One was hoping for better things, but there it is. I'll just have to lead on Algy Merriweather and his capers with a top model at Goodwood.'

'It's a tough world.'

'Does this mean the end of our prospective joint byline? If so, I'll have my ballpen back. It doesn't seem to have brought you much luck.' Seeing his hand go to his breast pocket, she waved him away. 'Keep it, Michael. I've a feeling it could still do things for you.'

'All this and a forgiving nature, too.'

She waved aside some of the smoke. 'What did you do to your hand?'

'Been chewing my nails and overdid it. Don't despair, Dulcie. Between us, we'll uproot a political scandal yet.'

'Of course we shall. 'Bye, Michael. Take care.'

Down in the street, a hammer blow from the sun flattened him against the *Clarion*'s stone façade, from which he detached himself with all the zest of a narcotics addict hurrying off to find work. Reaching for the painkillers, he stopped himself. Sooner or later his skull would have to be on its own, and for the sake of mental clarity it might as well be sooner. As things stood, it was an effort to recall the location of his own lock-up garage. For a moment he was tempted to forget about the hired Cortina. Then he remembered the last time he had started to rely on public transport, and in a mood of dull acceptance he set out on the four-street trudge to mobility. On the way, he bought a box of soft-centred chocolates for Lyn.

★   ★   ★

Leaving the Cortina in the driveway, he covered half the distance up the flagged path leading to the house before halting and turning back. Unlocking the double door to the garage, he heaved it up. Lyn's Metro was inside. He ran the Cortina in alongside it and lowered the door. The operation made quite a noise. He hoped the girls might hear and come tumbling out.

The rectangular, pleasant hall of the house looked neater than usual. His spirits took a further dip. A tidy house was a bad sign. The central rug, habitually askew or crumpled, had been flattened over the parquet, he noticed, and arranged square to the walls. Inside the cloakroom, garments were hung scrupulously on pegs. For once, he was able to find a place easily for his jacket instead of slinging it over a chair.

To judge from the general orderliness, he was in real trouble this time. Taking a breath, he went through to the lounge.

The room was empty, the furniture unrumpled. Crossing the Hoovered carpet to the glass sliding doors, he stared out at the garden. Alison's green-and-silver bicycle was propped against the pear tree; Caroline's doll's pram was parked by the rockery. Sparrows and starlings were hopping about the lawn.

The kitchen stood in disuse. Its condition was less immaculate than elsewhere. Some unwashed dishes lay on the drainer; a plastic carrier bulging with groceries leaned from a stool against the breakfast bar. Automatically he tested the topmost slab of butter with his fingers. It yielded squashily. As he was taking it across to the refrigerator, he spotted the message.

It was typed on a large sheet of vellum paper anchored by a china beaker to the adjoining worktop. Since leaving the *Clarion*'s accounts section to have the twins, Lyn had barely touched a keyboard. With a sensation of obscure alarm he grabbed up the sheet and found that it was two sheets, stapled at the north-west corner. The text was spaced single and a half. There was no salutation. The top line read:

If you want to see your family again, follow carefully the instructions below.

CHAPTER TWELVE

George Pershaw's voice was half an octave higher than normal. 'What's changed your mind, Mike? Something even bigger come up?'

'Could be.'

'Can't we at least have a foretaste? You said you might feel like flying a kite. I'll settle for that, Mike. We must have—'

'Will you listen? I can't do it ... not yet. I need time.'

'Just this morning you promised it by Friday. Second place is nowhere, remember. What if the *Record* catches a whiff of something and sends spies out? Either we—'

'I don't think you need worry about the opposition.'

'I needn't? My, that's a relief.' The news editor's irony trundled down the line with road-roller delicacy. 'Nice to have the Willoughby warranty on that.'

'You've trusted me before.'

'When you talk in that vein, Mike,' said Pershaw after a silence, 'you make things difficult. Naturally I've faith in you . . .'

'Then show some.'

Breath was sucked in at the far end. 'Okay, Mike. I'm not happy, but . . . okay. We'll hold our horses, on condition that you keep me informed.'

'As and when I can. There may be some delay.'

'How long?'

'A few days. I don't know.'

'I'll look forward to hearing from you.' The irony was diluted with resignation. The line went dead.

Mike dropped the receiver. He was shaking all over. Returning to the lounge, he thrust open the sliding door of a cabinet and grabbed a bottle and tumbler. The brandy scoured his throat before reaching his stomach in a ferment, sending shock-waves through his system. Pouring more, he splashed in soda and took the tumbler back to the kitchen, placing it alongside the typed message which he had transferred to

151

the breakfast bar.

Before hoisting himself on to the stool he went to the sink, ran the cold tap and put his head beneath it. The cool liquid impact brought gasps from him. Having swamped his face and hair, he dried off vigorously with a rough towel, scarcely aware of the pain from his bandaged hand. Combing his hair back, he took a number of deliberate breaths, inducing slight giddiness which he let pass while he stood motionless at the kitchen window, staring unseeingly at the sunlit landscape. Returning finally to the stool, he took another gulp from the tumbler, picked up the sheet of paper and reexamined the script.

★　　　★　　　★

Shortly after five, the telephone blurted in the hall.

'Mike? It's Becky. Would the girls feel like coming along for an hour or two, do you think? Jimmy's—'

'They're out with Lyn at the moment, I'm afraid.'

'Oh. Just my luck. Will they be long?'

'I don't think they'll be back for a while. I'll tell Lyn you called.'

'Okay, thanks.' Becky sounded a little nonplussed. 'How are you, Mike? Still sleuthing around like mad?'

'Keeping at it,' he said. 'Nice to hear from

you, Becky. Jimmy k-k-keeping fit?'

'Except for chronic boredom. Look in on us some time.'

'I'll do that. 'Bye for now.'

'Okay, 'bye,' she said rapidly, as if caught on the edge of a further remark.

Back in his lounge chair, Mike took another uncomprehending look at the *Custodian* crossword. One word, *Beefeater*, had been entered for Five Across. The block capitals were his own, but he couldn't remember writing them. He sat holding the fibretip, letting it form aimless outlines on the left-hand margin. When he looked up, his gaze met the bright eyes of the twins from their gilt frames on the lid of the baby grand piano. He had already tried reversing the photographs. It had made things worse, much worse.

After the early evening news bulletin, he tried to eat.

All that went down was half a cup of sweetened tea, which afterwards sat like slowly setting concrete on his abdomen while the food stayed untouched on the tray. For diversion, he tried to recall what the news bulletin had been about. A strike? Some disruption at the ports. A warning from somebody about something... Britain's competitive position in world markets ... the phrase had stuck in his brain, but it could have been from yesterday or even last week. Somebody else, now, was talking about

153

things that had occurred in the South-East. He allowed the voice to continue, because the alternative was silence.

A throbbing started up in his hand. Carrying the tray back to the kitchen, he found a pair of scissors and began carefully to remove the dressing, which seemed to have become too tight for the flesh. When he got to the wound, its messiness jolted him a little. Dropping the blood-soaked gauze into the waste bin, he found Lyn's first-aid box and made an amateur but less bulky job of binding himself up again, taking pains with the finishing off, glad of the occupation. While he was struggling one-handed with the ultimate knot, the telephone rang again.

'Oh hullo, Mike,' said the absurdly youthful voice of Lyn's mother. 'I didn't mean to disturb you—I was hoping to speak to Lyn. Is she within range?'

'She's out with the girls this evening.'

'Somebody's party, I suppose. It's not important. I just thought I'd find out how you all are and whether Lyn and the twins can possibly meet me in Reigate tomorrow morning. Do you think you could ask her?'

The bandage was starting to slip, causing a fresh seepage of blood over the telephone stand. Mike held his hand clear. The functioning vestige of his brain spun for a moment before rocking to a standstill, leaving a syllabic deposit

154

on his tongue.

'They won't be back tonight. The girls are sleeping at their friends'. Special treat.'

'Goodness, what a thrill. Lyn too?'

'No. She's taking the opportunity to visit an old ... office chum. I'm not quite sure when she'll be back.'

'I see. You'll be on your own, then.'

'I've some work to get on with.'

'How's it been going lately?'

'Fine.' Bloodspots were appearing on the hall carpet. Toppling an old directory off the stand with a knee, he kicked it into place to receive the drips.

'Well, don't oversleep in the morning. Like me to give you a call?'

'Not necessary, thanks. I'm always awake early.'

'All right, if you say so. Tell Lyn... No, I'll be phoning her later.'

'I should leave it till Friday. I think she's p-planning to do some shopping in Town.'

'I'd be very surprised if she wasn't,' Lyn's mother said drily. 'Good night, then, Mike. See you soon.'

Re-cleaning the wound under the kitchen tap, he dried it and replaced the bandage, clamping it with a safety-pin. When he had finished, the throbbing had abated and he could move his fingers. During the operation he tried to re-scan the exchange with Lyn's mother and found that although he could recall the dialogue he was incapable of assessing its tone in retrospect. He believed, though he couldn't be certain, he had kept command of his voice throughout. She had rung off without apparent misgivings. Returning to his chair in the lounge, he let the images from the TV screen flicker on the fringe of his consciousness.

At ten-fifteen, midway through another news bulletin, he went and prepared a fresh meal. Taking it back with him, he placed it carefully on a small table next to the armchair and forgot about it. A chat show followed the news, and then there was a programme about wildlife. After the shutdown he put his head back and closed his eyes.

Lyn's face whirled at him, frozen in a soundless scream. He sat up, sweating, trembling. Presently he rose and prowled the room on jellied legs. The moon, almost full, brushed the garden with a warm spectral frost. He went out to the kitchen, looked around vacantly, wandered down the hall, glanced into the cloakroom, came back to the lounge. Lyn's cassette-player stood on its rack near the sliding doors; picking out a selection from *Evita*, he played it at top volume while leaning against the double-glazing, staring out at the livid turf.

At two a.m. he stopped playing music and sat upright on the sofa in the deathly silence of the night.

At five o'clock he forced a slice of toast into himself.

After the third cup of coffee he washed and dried the china before dragging himself upstairs. Undressing clumsily, he sank into a warm bath, holding the bandage clear of the water, remaining tensely submerged for five minutes and then climbing out in a convulsion of urgency although it was not yet six. He dressed again with a complete change of clothing and ran the electric shaver across his face. His head, he noted with faint surprise, no longer protested when he stooped. His mind felt clearer than it had for days.

When the newspapers arrived at seven he had been pacing the hall for an hour. Snatching them from the doormat, he took them through to the lounge, found the *Custodian's* Personal column and spread it across the polished surface of the dresser. His eyes skidded down the line of type, taking in nothing. He forced himself to start again from the top.

Johnny, Barbados, '74, write Y. Thanks to St Nicholas. Malefactor, cry for always, Peacock . . . The mindless entries gave him his usual sensation of clawing at dream walls, heaving at rock-filled balloons. *Mimi ILY no roses now, constraint, MPD . . .* How could a reputable newspaper accept such drivel? *MW congratulations, call soon . . .*

His index finger halted. He re-read the line. *Call soon, office code plus 3832.* Using Dulcie's ballpen, he ringed the insertion and took the newspaper to the telephone.

After dialling he held the receiver tight to his ear, letting the ringing persist until the equipment called it off. He kept trying at three-minute intervals. Shortly after nine, he heard milk bottles being left at the door. When he went outside to collect them he met the postman.

'Not a lot for you, Mr Willoughby.'

Mumbling something, he retreated indoors. A buff window-envelope. A postcard for Lyn, from Susan in Austria. Some junk mail. Throwing it on the hallstand, he lost grip of a milk bottle and watched it smash against the far wall, distributing its contents with liberal abandon. Ignoring the mess, he went back to the telephone, dialled again.

The receiver at the other end was lifted.

He waited and then said, 'This is Mike Willoughby.'

'Please adopt the following procedure. Drive to the station. Leave your car there. Take the train to London. Wait in the concourse.'

The voice, though light-timbred, was probably male. Mike said, 'What about my family? Are they all right?'

158

He tried again. 'I've followed orders. Now you play fair with me. What about my wife and children?'

'Please adopt the following procedure. Drive to—'

Dropping the receiver, he went outside to the garage.

Finding a vacant bay in the station car park, he left the Cortina there and crossed by footbridge to the booking hall. It was occupied by a few commuter stragglers and a contingent of cheap-day shoppers. He saw no one he recognized, but the *Custodian* acted as a shield until the train arrived and continued to provide that service during the journey. Throughout, he stared at the same headline. Something to do with car production. No connection with reality.

He was first through the barrier. On all sides, holidaymakers stood in restive heaps; everywhere he looked, Alison and Caroline were skipping around suitcases. In one instance his certainty sent him scuttling towards a group, startling the parents, having to proceed past them in a pretence of making for a news stand as the ludicrous extent of his error became obvious. One of the youngsters was a boy, and the other was aged about five. Circling the news stand, he back-tracked to the barrier to stand for a while near his original point of exit.

Music wailed from the terminus roof. Lyn

kept glancing at him. Every slim, crop-haired woman who looked in his direction sent his heart lurching against his ribs. Presently he found it impossible to stand. Making for some seats, he found a vacancy between two groups and sat for a few moments, regaining some strength, before returning hurriedly to his former post, seized by a terrible conviction that he should have been there all along. The instruction had been precise ... or had it? *Concourse* could mean virtually anything. Weak-kneed, he approached the ticket-collector.

'Is this the only barrier, or is there another main concourse somewhere else?'

The collector, a coloured man with a beard, eyed him with tolerant amusement. 'She ain't showed up? Ain't no other tracks I know of. You stick around, she'll be along.'

Mike turned away. His feet took him to a new point twenty yards from the collector's view; the area was relatively a backwater, peopled only by himself and a thickset young woman seated alone on a baggage trolley, reading a paperback. Intent on keeping his distance from her, he experienced vague annoyance as she rose and walked towards him. In passing, she spoke across her shoulder.

'Follow me, please.'

Her cotton tunic outfit was an attractive shade of green: the surmounting platinum hair, done in pageboy style, bounced slightly as she walked

160

ahead of him through the arched exit to the taxi rank. Undeviatingly she made for a cab with its flag down, parked in the standing area. Opening the rear door, she waited for Mike to get in and joined him on the seat. Without instruction, the driver took the vehicle away into York Road and over Waterloo Bridge.

Mike relaxed his limbs into the upholstery. 'You've forgotten the blindfold.'

'That won't be necessary.'

She spoke with a polite detachment that discouraged further comment. They travelled at a routine pace towards Euston; the back of the driver's head gave an impression of calm maturity that was not belied by his roadcraft. From Camden Town the cab pursued an unveering course northwards. The woman next to Mike—she was older than he had first thought—sat with her fingertips in her tunic pockets, either preoccupied or on the verge of a doze. The cab's motion was sedative. She took no notice when he opened a window.

After twenty-five minutes the driver turned off into a district new to Mike. Active shopfronts gave way to derelict ones, which in turn yielded to small factories and warehouses: these tailed off finally at a point where the street became a semi-urban lane, a mere asphalt strip between belts of scrubby wasteland whose near horizons were tall chimneys and the forlorn backs of commercial buildings. To the right, a

161

stagnant canal gashed the terrain. A man was exercising two greyhounds along its nearer bank.

The cab slowed, bucking as it mounted a yellow-striped hump in the lane. Crawling a few more yards, it vaulted a second hump. To the left loomed a sign: MAX. SPEED 5 mph.

A gateway without a gate led into a drive of packed stones and gravel, festering with giant weeds. It followed an elliptical route alongside what might once have been a grassed expanse and was now a tangled wilderness, throttling its earstwhile border of shrubs and conifers. At the head of the drive, a single-storey prefabricated building sprawled under a canopy of variegated trees. It resembled a planter's bungalow, with corrugated metal roofing and a verandah. As the driver braked, Mike noticed another sign attached to the balustrade: VISITORS MUST REPORT TO RECEPTION.

He gave it a nod. 'Does one have a choice?'

Leaving the cab first, the woman held the door for him. He climbed out stiffly, hearing his knees crack: as he set his right foot down, the ankle gave way. She waited patiently while he flexed it back to strength, then preceded him to the verandah steps. Behind them, the cab drove off.

Inside, there was no reception area. Flaking paintwork of a grimy cream decorated the ante-room, which led immediately to a passage between partitioned offices: the upper halves of the partitions were of reeded glass. Linoleum of a dull mustard shade covered floorboards that echoed under their feet. This noise apart, the place was silent. The door to each office was closed and there was no hint of activity beyond the glass.

The passage ended in a wall of solid concrete housing a steel door. There was no sign of a lock or handle. Unzipping a pocket of her tunic, the woman produced a plastic card which she fed into a metal slit set into the concrete at shoulder-level. Folding her arms, she waited.

'Seems an unlikely place,' said Mike, 'for a cash dispenser.'

She disregarded the remark. A whine intervened: the steel door began to slide to the right. When it was fully open she gestured him through, pausing to extract the plastic card before following him into the small, steel-lined room whose sole equipment was a console of buttons just inside. She stabbed one with a thumb.

Presently the door whined back into place and a light came on. The floor fell away beneath them.

Catching up with it, Mike tried to camouflage his outward breath. Before his lungs had emptied, the floor pressed back against his feet and he had to snatch another breath to compensate. Beside him, the woman had

163

remained impassive. He was beginning to dislike her.

Another steel door slid back. They stepped out into a broad corridor, neon-lit, with ceramic-tiled walls and rubber flooring. The hum of air-conditioning was perceptible. Keeping pace with his guide, Mike felt they were descending the most gradual of gradients, but he guessed this might be illusory: the sensation was compounded by the corridor's steady curve to the right. They reached a junction with a still broader thoroughfare that accommodated steel doors at ten-yard intervals. Pausing at the third door along, the woman pressed another button. Overhead, a red light glowed.

Within seconds it changed to amber. The door rolled aside, giving access to a second steel-walled chamber with ceiling vents. Shut in by the door as it closed, they stood side by side while a sound like that of a household vacuum-cleaner roared from the vents, rose to crescendo and died abruptly. Except for a faint vibrancy, Mike had felt nothing.

Disorientation attacked him. Against his inclination he turned to the woman, who gave him a reassuring, wait-a-second flap of a manicured hand.

After some delay, the steel wall facing them began to divide with a distant rumble. As the gap increased, a vast room was exposed, its perimeter banked with computer machinery and radar screens, its centre housing raised surfaces bearing immense contour maps of coastlines and ocean approaches. Men and women in Service uniforms, of various ranks, moved unhurriedly between the equipment. Nobody glanced up as Mike and his guide left the chamber and walked the length of the room: the agitation-threshold of the place was impressively high. Here and there, one or two muted conversations seemed to be occurring, but the salient sound was the drone of the air-conditioning.

At the far end of the room, an open doorway led to a small flight of steps that culminated in a door of grained mahogany. The woman thumbed another button and waited.

Mike tried once more. 'Seems you need a lot of push around here.'

Nothing disturbed her features. He was about to add something less amiable when the door was opened by a blond, youngish man who stepped back to admit Mike to a plum-carpeted room containing a pair of desks and several easy chairs, and a second man who came forward with a smile and an outstretched hand. 'How nice to meet you, Mr Willoughby. I'm an avid reader of yours. I do hope we haven't put you to too much inconvenience.'

Mike accepted the hand. 'On the contrary, Prime Minister. You got me here with the minimum of fuss. But then of course, it's not myself I'm concerned for.'

CHAPTER THIRTEEN

'No cause for alarm. Your family is perfectly safe.'

'I must say, I was feeling more confident every second. But last night was a bad time. I take it there was a good reason for leaving me so totally in the dark?'

At a signal from the Prime Minister, the blond assistant pushed an easy chair against the back of Mike's knees, nudging him into it. The woman who had brought him was gone, he noticed. With a headshake he declined the offer of a cigarette, waited while Langholme selected one for himself and received a light from the assistant before returning to his chair behind the more central of the desks. To his right, maps and charts were pinned to the panelled wall; to his left, a number of plump volumes rested on shelves. The desktop bore nothing except two telephones, one coffee-brown, the other crimson. Adding a heavy glass ashtray to its deck cargo, the assistant retired silently to the other desk in a corner.

'I regret it very much,' said the Prime Minister, blowing smoke. 'It ran counter to every requirement of common humanity. Quite

166

simply, it was a matter of time. It was the only way we could be sure of keeping you quiet for another twelve hours or so until we could arrange to get you here. We had to act fast.'

'Why?'

'Because our information was that you were about to write a story which we should much prefer to remain unwritten.'

'The *Clarion*'s not out till Sunday.'

'No: but once your copy reached your news editor and the subs' desk, nothing could have prevented the investigation from gaining momentum. Am I right?'

Mike considered the matter. 'I suppose so. Where did you get your information?'

'You won't mind,' Langholme suggested, 'if we leave that for the moment? The vital thing was to halt your typewriter. In that we succeeded.'

'You certainly did, but why? If you think I was poised to touch off dynamite, you flatter me.'

The lean cheeks of the Prime Minister creased to make space for a grin. 'Flattery isn't my business, Mr Willoughby. Realism is. Hard facts tell me that when someone of your journalistic calibre starts the ball rolling, it really doesn't matter whether what's published is concrete or codswallop: either way, the damage is done. Fleet Street gets the signal and before we know it, everyone's sniffing the stench of another Watergate. Anyhow, I'm not convinced by your disclaimer.'

Mike regarded him thoughtfully. 'Wouldn't it have been easier on all concerned to have invited me round to Number Ten for a briefing? I don't think I'm generally regarded as unapproachable. I've reliable contacts in many a department, and one reason for this is that I'm known to respect confidences. If there's a good reason for information to be classified, I'll always pass it on to my superiors.'

'Naturally I considered that. Two factors argued against it. One I've already mentioned: time. A few more hours and your article, speculative or whatever, would have reached your news desk and the printing press, and that would have been that.' Langholme flicked ash. 'And secondly. Suppose that after being briefed you'd concluded that there was *no* sound reason for the information to be classified? Your editor might have decided to publish anyway, and to hell with D-notices.'

'What you're saying is, you don't trust us.'

'Where national security is at stake, I jib at placing my entire faith in anything or anybody.'

'So you deemed it justifiable to kidnap three innocent—'

'It's all been explained to them,' the Prime Minister said mildly. 'They're under no duress, I promise you.'

'When can I see them?'

168

'The moment we've had our chat. They're perfectly comfortable, and by now your wife will have been told that you know they're safe. As for your delightful twins, I understand they're treating this as a welcome break in the holiday tedium.'

'I can't think why it's not mandatory,' Mike said flintily, 'for everyone of school age. Abduction on the State: just one more loss-making nationalized industry. Well, Prime Minister, you may regard your motives as valid but in my opinion they stink. And leaving ethical considerations aside, what have you really achieved? I'm to leave here, it seems, fully primed, reunited with my family, in a position to spill any number of beans should I feel inclined. How does it alter things?'

Langholme sat back. 'I think I can best answer that question by taking events in chronological order. Do you know where you are, by the way?'

Mike shrugged. 'At a guess, a top-secret command post for use in a nuclear war.'

'Close enough. Without any desire to be theatrical, I thought it might be an apt place for us to meet, especially as I myself can come here without arousing comment—it's virtually an annexe to Downing Street. My visits are routine. But I also wanted you to have a glance at the place before hearing what I have to say. It might emphasize its importance.'

'I am always prepared to give due weight to what I hear.'

'Then we understand one another.' The Prime Minister beamed. 'Well now. The Godimer case. This is what you came to learn about?'

'I came to track down my family. But Godimer holds the key, obviously. Shall I tell you what I half-expected as I came through that door?'

'Please do.'

I thought I might find Patrick Godimer waiting for me.'

The Prime Minister sat up. 'You mean, you don't believe he's dead? That's a point of view I hadn't allowed for. However, I'm glad to say you're wrong, Mr Willoughby.'

'Glad?'

'Yes, indeed. I can say with absolute certainty that Mr Godimer is no longer alive, because it's I who arranged for him to be killed.'

*　　*　　*

'You'll have to give me a minute. I'm just letting that trickle in. You ... arranged it?'

'Most certainly. And very cleanly and efficiently were my orders carried out. My regard for the EPS has never been higher, I can assure you.'

'You used the Elite Personal Servce? Why not MI5?'

170

'They tend to be a little fastidious these days. Their way would have been to bring him to trial or send him into exile. Not good enough. Pat Godimer had to be removed from the scene and it had to be "accidental," Mr Willoughby. Do you understand now why your activities caused me vast concern?'

'I don't understand a thing. Why did Godimer have to be liquidated?'

'He was working against us.'

Mike gave a helpless laugh. '*Godimer*? He was building up our defences. He'd put muscle back into the Forces. What about Rainblast?'

'Rainblast . . . exactly.' The Prime Minister spoke quietly. 'What about that small thing?'

'Wasn't he about to get it for us from Washington? How the blazes would that help the Russians?'

'It wouldn't, of course. Not unless they were handed the secrets of the system, five years before they were due to discover them for themselves.'

Mike stared. 'You mean Godimer . . . ?'

'My long-standing friend and colleague, the Rt. Hon. Secretary of State for Defence,' Langholme said tightly, 'was planning to pass on details of the system to his Kremlin associates at the earliest practical opportunity.'

'You've got to be joking.'

'When I was told about it, given proof, Mr Willoughby, I never felt less like laughing.

Patrick and I went through university together. Climbed the same political ladder. He was one of us. Can you imagine how I felt?'

Mike drummed the desktop with his fingers. 'He'd been got at?'

'Very early on. As soon as he went up to university, I imagine; if not before. As you know, he was one of the Coverdale Set. A Right-wing caucus if ever there was one. And out of the lot of us, Pat seemed to be the most fiercely reactionary—sometimes even I was startled by the sheer venom of his tirades against the Left. All a charade. He'd been planted. Someone had made a shrewd guess at the likely composition of a future Rightist government and laid plans in good time.'

'So all the while Godimer was campaigning for the Right, getting elected . . .'

'He was simply biding his time.' The Prime Minister spoke with evident difficulty. 'For my part, I was being cultivated: there's no other way to describe it. Oratorical star of the Union, latent political force, best potential Right-wing Premier . . . all these tags were being sewn to my lapel at the time, and Pat made damn sure I took him along as part of the embroidery.' Langholme swallowed. 'I was happy to do it. He hoodwinked me from the start.'

'You and a few million others.'

'How could they have guessed? I'm the one

172

who swung him on them.'

'Which perhaps explains why you've now acted so decisively?'

Langholme's mouth twitched. 'Your phraseology is appreciated. Frankly, I had no choice.'

'What was your objection to bringing him to trial?'

'That must surely be obvious. Pat Godimer was instrumental in persuading the Americans to discuss making Rainblast available to us. Negotiations have reached a delicate stage. What would Washington's reaction have been if Britain's Defence Minister had suddenly been unmasked as a traitor? Can you see them saying, Oh well, here's Rainblast anyway, and best of luck? No chance. At the very least, they'd have clamped down for a few years while we overhauled our security. More likely, they'd have backed away from military co-operation for the foreseeable future, and who could blame them?'

'But can you be sure you've now eradicated the danger? After all, you trusted Godimer. Might there not be others in high positions who were working with him?'

The Prime Minister lobbed a meaningful glance to his assistant. 'A good point. There are no certainties in politics, no absolutes. All I'll say is this. A number of checks and balances are built into our system and the message did come through in the end. It applied to Godimer and no one else. The moment I was positive on that, I ... gave the order.'

Mike waited a moment. 'And with regard to the details, you're not proposing to enlarge?'

Langholme cocked an eyebrow. 'You're an investigative reporter, Mr Willoughby, with a talent for deduction. What would *you* say happened?'

'I'm willing to surmise on what didn't happen. For a start, I don't believe there was a fatal car crash.'

'Carry on.'

'I think Godimer's Jensen was brought to a halt less spectacularly than that. Some strategem: a "broken-down" van blocking the road ... something of that kind. After that we have a range of choices. A quick thump on the head from the "van driver". A jab from a hypodermic. Or maybe...' Mike paused. 'If we want to be really fanciful, how about a slug from a high-powered silenced rifle, aimed from a convenient nearby window?'

The silver-topped head of the Prime Minister tilted noncommitally. 'Quite imaginative.'

'Not quite. There does happen to be such a window. It belongs to a cottage that's inhabited by a gentleman who doesn't seem to belong to the neighbourhood ... he couldn't have been moved in for the occasion, by any chance? No, that can't be. How could it have been known that he might be needed, several months in advance?'

Their gazes met.

'A security investigation takes time, Mr Willoughby. Many months, as a rule. One would be failing in one's duty by not taking sensible pre-emptive measures. However...' Langholme hesitated. 'I'm bound to say, you're right about your own more fanciful speculation. That really does go a little over the top.'

'Let me just finish my little scenario. Let's assume the Jensen, one way or another, was brought to a standstill near the bend. We can then go on to assume that whoever then had the job of running the car over the side of the embankment was first obliged to remove Godimer from the driving seat—detaching his seat-belt in the process—so that the vehicle could finish up in the right spot. Once this had been done, rather than cram the Minister back behind the wheel, it was decided to spreadeagle him on the leaf-mould and leave the car door open, making it look as if he'd been flung out.'

The Prime Minister nodded judicially. 'Plausible.'

'Meanwhile, the van or truck that had blocked the road was driven up the track to the back of the cottage, out of sight. Peace then returned to the scene. It wasn't till early the following afternoon that somebody was sharp-eyed enough to spot the signs of a car having left the road, and discover the body.'

The Prime Minister said meekly, 'Why was it left to be found in that rather chancy way?'

'For authenticity. It had to be generally accepted as an accident. Therefore it was better if an ordinary member of the public was genuinely the first to report it.'

'But what if no one had?'

'By the following Monday, Godimer would have been missed. Then, of course, a search would have been launched and the wreck discovered.'

Langholme pondered. 'Not at all bad,' he said finally. 'I'm still not keen on the part about the rifle. Any reasonably sharp-eyed investigating police officer would have noticed, surely, that the cause of death was a bullet rather than contact with the dashboard.'

'So I'm wrong about the rifle. I don't think I'm mistaken about much else. Least of all the repercussions.'

'Repercussions?'

'The disposal of people like Alf Barnard and Dave Philcox, the villagers who were prepared to say they'd seen Godimer driving his car like a hearse a few minutes before the crash. Potentially embarrasing, that. Not in tune with the score.'

The Prime Minister frowned in perplexity at his assistant. 'Here, I've lost you, Mr Willoughby.'

'No, you haven't. I'm still around, this troublesome guy from the *Clarion*, poking into things best left undisturbed. Still alive and inquisitive, despite being shot at and having his brakes doctored. Do I sound a little touchy? I wouldn't want to give that impression. It's just that, while I can cheerfully accept professional rivalry, attempts on my life strike me as being outside the rules.'

Langholme studied him in silence. From his corner, the assistant said, 'I think Mr Willoughby's imagination is rather running away with him.'

'On the contrary, it's well in harness. If you really want me to—'

'A good journalist,' the Premier interposed, 'recognizes facts. The construction he places on those facts may be less infallible, but we needn't go into that now. My point is this. No one, to my knowledge, has tried to do you harm, Mr Willoughby. You have my personal assurance on that.'

'Then who's been setting me up?'

'That's an intriguing question.' Langholme made a sign to his assistant, who rose and left the room. 'One thing's clear. Neither of these alleged attempts on your life deterred you. Sunday's *Clarion* would have carried your story—*The Godimer Riddle*, or some such treatment. Am I right?'

'I can't anticipate editorial decisions.'

'Very proper,' the other said smoothly. 'But I think we can save you some troube. At the same time, you can do your country a favour and help me personally out of a dilemma. When Alan comes back I'll show you what I mean. Have you lived in Surrey long?'

'Six years.'

'Your wife likes it there?'

'Yes,' Mike replied tersely. 'The twins have a lot of friends.'

'Lively couple. You must be proud of them.'

'They suit me all right.'

The Premier smiled. 'Spoken like a British father. Well, I hope they haven't captivated their new friends in the EPS too severely, or there'll be some broken hearts when they leave. Let me repeat how sorry I am that you were given a night of such anxiety. It really was unavoidable.'

'Anything for patriotism.'

'It's hardly the kind of thing one would normally . . . Ah, Alan. Is that tea or coffee? No matter, it's sure to be excellent. We do ourselves well here, you know. The catering staff are hand-picked from the Senior Service. Pour a cup for Mr Willoughby, Alan, and let him have the envelope, will you?'

Mike took what he was offered. The envelope was buff manila, and felt empty. 'Take a look,' invited the Premier, his attention on the coffee-pot.

The envelope contained a single sheet of flimsy paper bearing half a dozen typed paragraphs. Mike scanned them before refolding the sheet and returning it to the envelope, which he placed carefully alongside the ashtray on the desk. The blond Alan handed him a cup and saucer. For an instant he poised the cup's rim at his lips, savouring the promise; then he took the first exquisite sip, expelling breath after doing so, as if on cue for a TV commercial.

'You're right,' he said. 'It's very good.'

'I'm sure you must be in need of it.'

Declining the offer of sugar, Mike sipped again. Nursing the cup, he stared unseeingly at the crimson telephone. 'The thing I'm most in need of,' he said, 'is a reunion with my family.'

'Absolutely. They're not here, unfortunately, since it hardly seemed the environment for a pair of small girls . . .'

'They'd have been thrilled to bits.'

'Well, perhaps. That never occurred to me. Anyway, they'll be back with you in no time at all.'

Mike drank a little more coffee, pushed the china away across the shining mahogany surface and got to his feet. 'Time I was leaving, then.'

The Premier rose also. 'Thank you for listening to what I had to say. I'm sure we both have a better understanding of the situation. Don't forget your envelope.'

'I shan't be needing that.'

'You're happy to rely on memory? Fine, but I'd be grateful if you wouldn't mind keeping as closely as possible to the suggested working. Just to avoid possible complications.'

'I think you misunderstand me, Prime Minister. I'm not taking the envelope because I've no intention of letting its contents be published. They're inaccurate. I don't lend my name to inaccuracy.'

Placing his fingertips on the desk, Langholme allowed them to support his weight for a moment while he stared down. Then he looked up.

'Can I ask you to resume your seat, Mr Willoughby? I think we'd better have another talk about this.'

Mike complied. 'We seem to have had quite an exchange of views already,' he remarked. 'Still, I'm the receptive type. I'm prepared to go on listening.'

'Good.' The Premier remained standing. 'For my part, Mike—you don't mind if I call you that?—I was never one to shirk harsh decisions, as you may have gathered. At the same time, I abhor any needless cracking of the whip. Tell me something. Knowing what you now know, why do you have this reluctance to help out in the way I've indicated?'

Mike reflected briefly. 'I trust this isn't going to sound pompous. Here goes, anyhow. I'm

Mike Willoughby of the *Clarion*. My career, if it amounts to anything, is based on two things: readability and reliability. I've never written a damn syllable I couldn't back up with facts. People trust me. How can you expect me to explode a lifetime's achievement with one shoddy cover-up?'

'What's shoddy about helping to safeguard your country?'

'Look. If it's that vital, why not issue those paragraphs in the form of an official handout? Leave me out of it.'

Unhesitatingly the Premier shook his head. 'Not good enough, Mike, I fear. A Whitehall statement ... what weight would that carry? Public scepticism mounts in direct ratio to official denials. What would your news editor say? "Number Ten discounts any funny business in the Godimer affair, Mike. What's your version?" And your reply? "Sorry, George, I don't have a version, my lips are sealed." Would he accept that?'

'I can't say. Does it matter?'

'It could. Others in Fleet Street might start thinking. A gag on Mike Willoughby? Must be something behind it. Wants looking into. This is the kind of thing that could happen. You know it is.'

'Okay, so it could happen. I can't prevent it.'

'Yes, Mike, you can. By running that story under your own name you can kill the rumours.

Willoughby says there's nothing in it: ergo, there's nothing in it. End of episode.'

'Flattery again. No single hack journalist carries that weight of punch.'

'I think you underrate yourself.'

From the corner came the soft clinking of crockery as Alan returned it to the tray. Apart from this and the ubiquitous purr of the air-conditioning, there was no sound in the room. The light dimmed under a load-surge before brightening again. It came as a necessary reminder that the place was underground.

'There's something I'd like to be clear about,' said Mike. 'Suppose I refuse to do what you're asking? What then?'

'In that event,' the Prime Minister replied slowly, 'the position would have to be reassessed with the greatest care.'

CHAPTER FOURTEEN

The house seemed musty. He opened a few windows to let in the sun-baked afternoon air, slid back the glass doors and stood briefly on the patio, feeling the warmth beat up from the flagstones. The lawn, he noted mechanically, needed cutting again. The twins' playthings were still as they had been left the previous day. Returning to the house, he went through to his study and uncovered the typewriter.

Seating himself before the machine, he selected paper and carbons and fed in the package. At the centre-top he typed 'Sheet 1' and in the right-hand corner 'Willoughby.' Reaching into his inside pocket, he produced the manila envelope, removed what it contained, spread it out and read it through. He shut his eyes for a moment, reopened them and started to prod at the keyboard.

Police and the security services are now fully satisfied that the death of the late Defence Minister, Patrick Godimer, was accidental.

Intensive investigations, I can reveal, have turned up nothing sinister relating to the Kent car smash in which the Minister died. From their examination, experts have confirmed that Mr Godimer's Jensen Interceptor left the road— at a notoriously 'hairy' bend—because it was travelling too fast in gathering dusk.

There is no suggestion of recklessness. Mr Godimer, however, was known as a flamboyant motorist and had been involved in two previous accidents. There is no doubt in the minds of security chiefs that the Minister 'ran out of highway' on this occasion and met his death as a result. Evidence to be given shortly at the resumed inquest will bear out this analysis.

Leaning back, Mike contemplated the sheet

with half-closed eyes before indenting for an additional paragraph.

The Prime Minister, who was a personal friend of Mr Godimer, has paid tribute to his political achievements. And his appointment of Melvin Beattock as Mr Godimer's successor is taken by observers in Whitehall as an indication that there will be no change in existing defence policy. Although untested in high office, Mr Beattock is believed to be closely associated with the Premier's hawkish views and, it is confidently expected, will pursue the same objectives. He is particularly anxious to continue to foster Anglo/US co-operation.

Winding out the sheets, Mike separated the top copy and scrutinized the text. With a ballpen he excised the final word and substituted 'collaboration in the field of weapons technology.' He read the story once more. Then he picked up the extension telephone and dialled.

He asked for copy-transmit and was connected after a fifteen-second delay. With painstaking distinctness he dictated the paragraphs, waited for the concluding bleep of acknowledgement, and hung up.

Presently he went out to the kitchen and made himself toast and coffee. Taking the remnants of the toast out to the bird-table on the lawn, he went on to inspect the floral borders, plucking a weed here and there. He was surprised, on his return, to find a bunch of squashed greenery in his right fist; he dropped it inside the dustbin before re-entering the house, now ventilated and cool by comparison with the garden. Returning to his study, he cleared the stationery into a drawer and replaced the cover of the machine. Seated at the desk, he gazed vacantly through the window at the street.

The Bates family opposite were swarming into their Chrysler with picnic baskets and dogs. There was a good deal of shouting and door-slamming before the car took off noisily, alive with tumbling figures. When it was gone, silence fell back like a turned mattress. Mike walked out of the study and into the lounge, where he switched on the television.

A tennis match was in progress. Thunderous applause from the crowd, acclaiming a rally, swamped the room for a few moments, obliterating other sound. When it subsided, he was able to hear the ringing of the telephone in the hall. Silencing the set, he strode outside.

'Mike? This story you've just sent over. I'm assuming it's intended as some kind of a joke.'

'No joke, George. That's the outcome of my enquiries.'

During the ensuing pause he could hear the distant clash of metal, the hum of machinery.

'You expect us to print this?'

'That's up to you.'

'Listen, Mike. I went along with you yesterday, didn't I? You asked for more time. I agreed you could have it. My reason for agreeing was that I trusted you to be as good as your word and come up with something at least controversial, even if it was this side of megaton capacity.' Pershaw paused again, breathing audibly. 'What's got into you? Has somebody threatened your life again?'

'Nobody's threatened my life.'

'So you're seriously telling me this is the story you'd like printed under your byline?'

'I wouldn't have phoned it otherwise.'

'Take a jump. We'll get more mileage out of Nicki Randall's kiss-and-tell diaries. Excuse me while I go and produce a newspaper. We'll talk later.'

'Wait, George. Don't hang up. I want you to run that story, it's ... very important. Still there? It's vital it should appear.'

When Pershaw spoke again, his tone had altered subtly. 'I'm just reading it over. You say the police and security top brass are satisfied. You don't say anything about yourself. Are *you* satisfied?'

'I shall be if you print it.'

'As it stands?'

'As near as possible.'

'And that's it? No follow-up?'

'That's ... debatable at present.'

'Who's debating? Are you still on the story? Do I sit back to await further instalments or don't I? You've got to put me in the picture, Mike.'

'It's too delicate right now.'

There was no immediate reply from Pershaw, who seemed to have gone away. Mike could still hear the clatter of machinery. He said 'George?' experimentally, twice. After the repetition the news editor's voice came back, enunciating carefully.

'Because of who you are, Mike—because of this crass confidence I've always had in you, stemming from past exploits—I intend to take you on trust. Okay? I'm going to run this hunk of sterile garbage verbatim in bold type on the front, as you request. And I hope to God it's not the outcome of brain damage.' Another pause. 'How do you feel, incidentally?'

'I'm all right, George, believe me.'

'Why shouldn't I believe you? I've swallowed everything else.'

'Thanks. You won't regret it.' Mike's hand started to tremble uncontrollably as he lowered the receiver.

*　　*　　*

'You only just caught me, Mr Willoughby.' The green eyes observed him speculatively. 'I was

187

about to leave for Windsor. Are you making any progress?'

'I'd appreciate it, Lady Tessa, if we could talk.'

She glanced at her watch. 'Well, the car's waiting, but ... Won't you sit down? I'd offer you tea, but Sally's not here today and I don't—'

'No tea, thanks.' Mike slumped on to the sofa. She sat on the arm of a nearby chair, watching him closely.

'Something's wrong?'

'Everything. That's why I've come to you.'

'What can I do?' Her voice was ironically self-deprecating. 'I'm nobody now, you know. If I ever was.'

'You were Pat Godimer's wife for nine years. Did you ever question his loyalty?'

She stared. 'To the Party, you mean?'

'Not to the Party. Did you ever see him as a traitor to his country?'

She let out a brief, uncertain laugh. 'You've been talking to the lunatic Left. Is that it? Don't tell me you take seriously a word they say.'

Mike shook his head.

Traces of impatience seeped into her posture. 'May I take it, Mr Willoughby, you've not had too successful a week? Your deadline's near and you've nothing to show for your efforts? But there's still a chance to carry some sensational utterance from the widow of the month. *My Turncoat Husband, by Wife of Spendthrift*

188

Minister . . .'

'I wouldn't dream of it, Lady Tessa.' His voice remained flat. He was incapable of varying its inflection in any way. Her anger seemed to disperse.

'Whatever you may have been told—discount it. Pat had his faults, goodness knows. He didn't always listen to advice, for one thing. But *treason*? That's grotesque. Ask anybody. Put it to any single—'

'I don't have to.' He glanced at her. 'Will it please you to know, Lady Tessa, that Sunday's *Clarion* will carry a front-page story by me, informing the world that no suspicion is attached to the circumstances of his death?'

She frowned. 'That's the official line. You go along with it?'

'I have to.'

Extracting a small lace handkerchief from a sleeve, she began polishing the face of her wristwatch. 'I'm not sure I quite understand. I thought you were a free-ranging, open-minded newsman, guided entirely by your own—'

'Lady Tessa,' he interrupted, 'I'm having pressure put on me. The story isn't mine. It comes from Whitehall, and it's a cover-up.'

'Only to be expected,' she said scornfully, replacing the handkerchief. 'Nobody wants to rock the boat. Except people like yourself, I thought. Surely you don't intend to let it rest, merely because an official treacly statement has been handed out?' She paused, eyeing him. 'Pressure? What kind of pressure?'

'I'm a family man. Family men are vulnerable.'

Her eyes widened. 'If you mean what I think you mean . . .'

'There's no point in beating about the bush. Unless that story appears on Sunday, word for word . . .' Suddenly he was breathless. 'Unless it's printed, I don't know when I shall see my wife and children again.'

'What on earth are you saying?'

'They're officially in protective custody. I've no idea where.'

She gazed at him speechlessly.

'Mind you,' he added, 'it was done most apologetically. I can't complain about the remorse that's on display. At the same time, I've been left in no doubt whatever of the consequences of any deviation—now or in future. The smallest lapse, and there'll be a case rigged against me to deprive me of my marital rights. Evidence would be concocted, my wife would be turned against me and I'd probably be banned from seeing the kids.'

'I don't believe it,' she said faintly. 'Who made this threat?'

'It came from the top.'

'Ralph? Has he taken leave of his senses?'

'He seemed well in control. If not, I'd have gone elsewhere to blow the whole thing, despite the risk to myself. But I'm up against the Establishment. They're intent on writing history as they want it, and to hell with anyone who tries to interfere.'

Lady Tessa gripped the back of the chair. 'This history they're writing. How does it read?'

'It casts your late husband as a Kremlin mole from his university days. And it says he was planning to pass details of Rainblast, the anti-missile system, to the Russians.'

Fury suffused her face, to be joined almost instantly by bewilderment. 'It's a wicked lie,' she said in a strangled voice, 'but if through some madness they thought it was true, why the cover-up?'

'They're afraid that if the truth gets out, Washington will lose all remaining faith in our security and refuse to sell us Rainblast.'

'The truth,' she repeated. She looked at him with venom. 'You're convinced my husband *was* a spy, Mr Willoughby?'

'I'm convinced of nothing. My enquiries are only half-complete. Up until today I'd drawn no conclusions, and now I'm finding it hard to think. I've other things on my mind.'

'In that case...' Lady Tessa went to an antique sideboard and extracted a bottle and a couple of glasses. 'First of all, I think we both need a stimulant. And secondly...' Unstopping the bottle, she began pouring. 'Leaving everything else aside, wouldn't it be better from your point of view to simply go along with them? Let that story appear on Sunday, get your family back, do nothing more about it? It's Whitehall's problem, not yours. How can you take the risk of losing your wife and children?'

'Because,' Mike said hoarsely, 'I have this weird feeling that it could end up as everyone's problem.'

★   ★   ★

As they left the car, there was time for him to absorb a quick impression of a genuine Georgian façade before they passed through a colonnaded entrance into a close-carpeted reception hall, slantingly lit by the setting sun via emerald-curtained windows in the west wall. Lady Tessa led him through to a rear drawing-room overlooking an unkempt lawn that sloped away to a conifer hedge in the middle distance. A pair of white-painted wrought-iron seats stood against the hedge to one side. The overall effect was stately in a faintly raffish manner.

'Wait here. I'll call my father.' She left the room.

Mike went to the french door and looked out. A shabbily-dressed man with bowed shoulders, wearing a floppy cotton hat, was walking a wheelbarrow across the turf; watching his progress, Mike was put cloudily in mind of Alf

Barnard, the village handyman. The gardener vanished around the side of the house. Mike gave brief thought to the idea of sitting down and remained standing, observing the tall stone walls that bordered the grounds.

From the hall came the sound of voices, low-pitched, confidential. Lady Tessa reappeared, tailed by the man who had been pushing the wheelbarrow. 'Dad, this is Mike Willoughby of the *Clarion*,' she said. 'My father, Lord Manninge.'

They shook hands. The palm of the older man was slightly damp and extremely dirty. He looked Mike up and down.

'Tessa's just this minute given me the bare bones, Mr Willoughby. The part I can understand, I find somewhat incredible. Would you mind taking a seat over there and fleshing the story out for me a little?'

Mike did as he was asked. At the end of his account there was a short silence, broken by Lady Tessa. 'Do you think Ralph can somehow have been tipped over the edge?'

Lord Manninge's head, now unswathed, commenced a rhythmic shaking. 'Not Ralph. He's always known exactly what he's about. I only spoke to him a couple of days ago. He was thoroughly in possession of his marbles.'

'Frightened, then?'

'He doesn't scare easily. But I'll admit, it does sound as if he knows he's dealing with something so crucial that . . . Whether it would excuse treatment of this sort . . . On the other hand, if he felt that national security—'

'Even then,' said his daughter.

'Yes, I have to agree with you.' Spitting on his hands, Lord Manninge rubbed them raspingly together to remove some of the filth. Finally he produced a handkerchief and began drying off each arthritic finger. 'Ralph,' he pronounced, 'is clearly a rattled man. Obviously he felt compelled to behave out of character on this occasion, which to me suggests one thing—he's faced with "X" the unknown and is having to improvise. There's no substance, of course, in this threat of his. He was just trying to panic you, Mr Willoughby.'

'It wasn't a bad try,' his daughter observed tartly.

'So, after Sunday I can expect my family back, whether or not that story gets printed?'

Lord Manninge hesitated. 'I can't answer for day-to-day—'

'With respect, sir,' Mike said bluntly, 'I don't think you fully appreciate the position. The alternatives were spelled out to me. I was left in positively no doubt.'

The finger-wiping came to a halt. Lady Tessa's father pondered for a few moments.

'Then,' he said eventually, 'our esteemed Premier is evidently desperate, and I'd give a lot to know why.'

'If your son-in-law really was a Kremlin agent . . .'

Lord Manninge smiled. 'No question of that.'

'The Prime Minister was categorical about it.'

The older man nodded vigorously. 'Because he's been fed false data. High up in British Intelligence—that's where the danger lies. By some means or other, evidence has been planted to implicate Patrick as Moscow's stooge, and Ralph's fallen for it. Sorry, my dear. But it's obvious. Patrick was doing too good a job as Defence Minister. Moscow decided he must go, so they hatched this story about his supposed double-dealing and got it filtered through to Number Ten. Hoping that Ralph would be forced to do their nasty work for them. Which is just what he's done.'

'I've suspected something of the sort,' Lady Tessa said tightly, 'ever since it happened.'

'But for the Prime Minister to take such action,' Mike protested, 'he must have been given some pretty persuasive proof.'

'I'm certain he was. Someone in Intelligence—perhaps two or three of them, who knows?—has been adroit enough to fool everyone who matters, presumably for quite a while.' Lord Manninge sprang up, his knees crackling. 'This is going to need delicate handling. First, we have to convince Ralph that he and no doubt others in the Cabinet have been hoodwinked. Then he, in turn, will be faced

195

with the problem of rooting out the mole, or moles. And that's not going to be easy. What is it, Mr Willoughby?'

'Sir, are you planning to make direct contact with the Premier on this?'

'Of course I am. What other procedure do you suggest?'

'I must point out, the sole reason I was given the information was to convince me that a false story under my name in the *Clarion* was vital to the nation's security. If the Premier now discovers that I immediately went away and blabbed top secret details—'

'I wouldn't fuss yourself about that.'

'But what if you don't succeed in convincing him? It'll be your word against that of this highly-placed mole, whoever he is. And you've got an axe to grind—you were Pat Godimer's father-in-law. Why should the Prime Minister prefer your version?'

Lord Manninge looked disconcerted.

'Mr Willoughby could be right,' said Lady Tessa. 'Ralph can be stubborn, and without irrefutable proof...'

'He's got my family, don't forget. He could take it out on them.'

'Unthinkable.'

'This time yesterday,' said Mike, 'I'd have agreed with you.'

'If you feel this way,' said the peer with a touch of asperity, 'why did you go straight to my daughter this afternoon? You might have been seen.'

'I took a chance. I've taken a bigger one, coming here. I had to consult somebody.'

Lord Manninge strode decisively to the door. 'Stay here,' he ordered. 'I have to make a phone call.'

CHAPTER FIFTEEN

Lady Tessa came across to Mike as he sat staring lethargically at a picture of a mountain scene on the facing wall. 'I'm sure you've no cause to worry, Mr Willoughby.'

'You've faith in your father?'

'He has a great deal of influence.'

'So has the Press,' said Mike. 'Up to a point.'

'Give him another five minutes. If by that time—'

Lord Manninge returned, scowling. 'I can't get through. The line seems to be dead.'

Mike raised his head slowly to look at them both.

Lady Tessa recovered smartly. 'You'd better go out and try from a call-box.'

'Save your energy,' Mike advised.

'What?'

'They won't let you do it, Lord Manninge. Obviously they tailed me here. They know what

197

I'm aiming for.'

'I don't follow.' Lady Tessa's father looked perplexed and uneasy. 'What's to stop me walking to the nearest phone? I have to report the fault.'

'There's no fault.'

'What Mr Willoughby is saying,' Lady Tessa explained gently, 'is that the line has been tampered with. They're watching the house.'

'Who?' exploded Lord Manninge.

Mike stood up. 'Attractive garden of yours,' he observed with a nod of the head. 'Keeps you busy, I imagine. How far does it stretch?'

Lord Manninge twisted from the waist to regard the lawn with a kind of vacant semi-hostility. 'Hell of a way down to a copse. Why are we talking about gardens?'

'Is there a way out at the bottom?'

'If you like to hop over the stream. Look, what's the good of running off? As soon as I'm able to get through to Ralph—'

'You do things your way, Lord Manninge. I'll go mine.'

Wrenching open the french door, Mike stepped on to the terrace. Lady Tessa darted after him. 'Turn left,' she instructed, 'after you've crossed the stream. Follow the track until you reach an open space by the Memorial. You might get a bus from there. Good luck.'

Nodding thanks, Mike trotted across the lawn, following the flattened streak that betrayed the well-used route to the conifer hedge and beyond. At the centre of the grassed expanse a sense of vulnerability attacked him. Impulsively he ducked as he ran. Ahead of him, a little to his right, a wad of turf spurted with a thud.

Instinct howled at him to pull up. Instead he put on speed, throwing a leftward glance which showed him a glimpse of a black-clad hooded figure stationed amid foliage on top of the stone wall, some way to his rear. A residual ray from the sinking sun highlighted a glint of metal.

He started to zigzag. Deep within his throat, a pilot-light had been ignited and was comprehensively scorching the lining, causing incoming breath to sear his lungs. His legs felt ludicrously splayed. He was through the gap in the hedge. Some distance ahead lay trees, a mix of birch and larch. Straightening course, he made for them in a final dash. As he approached their fringe a second hooded form emerged to stand with weapon levelled.

With a shrug and a gesture he came to a halt.

As the figure advanced, he raised both arms. Gripped two-handed, the pistol never wavered. *I leave my heart in an English garden*... Suddenly he felt relaxed, limp almost. Indifference had overtaken him. Whatever happened, it didn't matter. Nothing counted for much. Human relationships aside, possibly. He did wish he and Lyn had managed to avoid quarrelling.

The figure paused. 'Snatch my gun.'

Mike cocked an enquiring head.

'Take the damn thing, will you?' Urgency ejected from the mouth-slit of the hood. 'Make it look good. Then get the hell out of here.'

'What's going on?'

'Something that shouldn't be—and you're the guy to expose it. Hit me!'

The pistol came enticingly within reach.

Mike's grab was half-hearted, but it earned him the prize. The outstretched arm yielded as he wrenched it back: the figure staggered, presenting its hooded crown as a target. Mike brought the pistol down, not hard. It connected sullenly with the hidden skull. The figure crumpled.

As he stood gazing down at it, two syllables jumped faintly from the ground. '*Beat it!*'

Throwing the gun aside, Mike headed for the stream.

★   ★   ★

The sandwich bar was having a quiet time. Nibbling at a ham roll on the end stool, he kept a covert check upon the few customers who came and went. One of them stood hesitant just inside the door, his eyes scanning the few tables to the left. Mike spoke in a low voice.

'Over here, Maurice.'

Trent jerked, blinked, came across, climbed

on to the adjoining stool. 'You chose a fine time,' he grumbled. 'They're debating the Defence Estimates.'

'I was afraid you hadn't got my message. Is someone deputizing for you?'

'Thomas is there. He's done Parliamentary work before. But you know, Mike, this had better be important. I was hoping to—'

'Skip the recriminations. I need your help, Maurice, badly. Tell me this: who in the Cabinet can be trusted absolutely?'

Trent looked nonplussed. 'To do what? Give a straight answer to a question?'

'I'm not talking of PR attitudes. Whose integrity is copper-bottomed? Who would you, personally, lay it on the line for?'

'Puttenham,' Trent said promptly.

'That's who I figured you'd say. Do you have a line to him?'

'We've been buddies for twenty years,' the *Clarion*'s political correspondent admitted with modesty.

'Do you know where he is right now?'

'He was still in the Chamber when I left. I assume he'll—'

'Is there a chance you can fetch him out of there to see me?'

Trent showed his amazement. 'You don't yank the Home Secretary out of his Front-bench seat during a key debate to buy him a coffee and a—'

'Please, Maurice. It's desperately urgent.'

Shooting a glance at the counter attendant, a small swarthy man who was rearranging food in a glass case and humming to Greek music on the radio, Trent dropped his voice. 'Is it Godimer?'

'What the hell do you think?'

'I'm not sure what to think,' Trent responded mildly. He slid from the stool. 'So perhaps I'll just try to do as you ask. It may take a little while.'

'I'll wait. If you can manoeuvre him along here without being noticed, I'll be ever in your debt. Oh—and Maurice. If you can't contact him, *don't* approach anyone else. Liaise with me first, okay?'

Through the window he watched Trent cross the road on the green signal and head back for Westminster. Once the lithe, erect figure was out of sight, it became hard to sit still. Muscles in various limbs kept twitching, as though independently urging action. He had been continuously on the move for some hours, and yet he felt no fatigue: every part of him was at red alert. He ordered another coffee from the attendant, who wore sideburns meeting under his chin. The man barely looked at him. The coffee was more pungent than ever, unless his tolerance of the poison was reaching its limit. He sat clasping the cup, not sipping.

The minutes congealed into an hour.

Restlessly Mike left the sandwich bar, took a stroll towards Westminster Bridge, keeping watch on the premises and turning before they were out of sight. Loath to re-enter the bar, he paced a short distance the other way, passing within a yard of a police constable and his female colleague who were stationed on the corner of Parliament Street in verbose radio communication with a Duckspeak voice, neither of them seemingly interested in their immediate surroundings. When he re-passed them on the way back they had extinguished the voice and were murmuring together at an intimate level. He felt that their joint gaze was fixed on his spine. He made himself amble.

Opposite the sandwich bar, the pedestrian signal was at green. On an abrupt decision he crossed the street, turning at the far side for a final look: he was in time to see two cars, their roof-mounted lamps discernible but unwinking, draw up silently outside the bar and disgorge a number of men in plain clothes who took up flanking positions across the pavement before starting to close in slowly. He watched them for a moment before walking on at an even pace.

Continuing in leisurely style to the further corner of Parliament Square, he again crossed the road and hailed a taxi that was cruising in the Victoria direction. 'Nowhere particular,' he told the driver. 'Just stooge around, will you, while I think about it.'

Midway along Victoria Street he made his decision.

CHAPTER SIXTEEN

The butler uttered on a note of finality. 'The Field Marshal is entertaining a party to dinner, sir. He can't be disturbed.'

'Go in and disturb him. Tell him it's Mike Willoughby of the *Clarion*. Tell him it's urgent.'

'Mr Willoughby on urgent business. I'm afraid that's really not sufficient. My instructions—'

'Waddle inside,' Mike snarled, 'and *make* it sufficient.'

The butler stepped back. 'The Field Marshal left strict—'

'I'll wait in this room, just here. If he's not with me in two minutes, I'll burst in and wreck the table.'

★   ★   ★

'Good evening, Mike. I hear you're being a little obstreperous.'

'Good to see you, Sir Robert. "Insistent" is the word I'd favour. Your butler stood his ground nobly, so I'm afraid I had to use intimidation. I hope you'll forgive me when you hear why.'

'I hope so, too. I've half the General Staff in there, stranded over the soup. What did you want to see me about?'

'Something you're not going to believe.'

'If that's the case,' the Field Marshal said testily, 'why go to the trouble of disrupting my social life? You know I've a lot of time for you, Mike. I've always respected your professionalism. And I don't forget what you've done in the past on behalf of the Armed Forces. Why else do you think I agreed to come out and see you? Now let's have it.'

For ten minutes he listened closely, his face expressionless. He put a question or two, pondered the answers, asked another question and finally went to the door. 'Give me half an hour,' he said curtly. 'Meanwhile you'd better stay here and keep out of sight.' His mouth sprang a quirk. 'Read a newspaper. There's usually something of interest.'

Mike sat on a hard chair, spread his legs and stared at the floor. Now, with the burden shifted, he did feel weary. Also the cranial discomfort was stealing back, threatening to dominate. He searched his pockets unsuccessfully for the painkillers. A night's rest was what he had needed. An hour would help. If Sir Robert's furniture had been more comfortable, nothing would have prevented the onset of sleep.

The return of the Field Marshal snatched him out of a dream. He sat up, groaning involuntarily as the headpain made a lunge. The wall-clock announced that nearly an hour had elapsed. Closing the door carefully, Sir Robert stood at ease against it and gave Mike a sober inspection.

'You were perfectly right,' he said.

Mike gestured tiredly. 'I knew I was. It was a question of proof.'

'Well, I've set the wheels in motion. We should have results quite shortly.' Compassion stole into the Field Marshal's gaze. 'Don't worry about your family. They're not at risk.'

'Where are they being held?'

'They'll be back with you before long. As for Lord Manninge and his daughter, they've been released from house arrest. I've assumed command and issued certain orders. I think we can expect the situation to stabilize within the next hour.'

Mike looked at him. 'A military coup? Here in Britain?'

'I suppose one might call it that.' The Field Marshal sounded unflustered.

'You think the country will buy it?'

'Oh, I don't anticipate much difficulty.' Sir Robert glanced at his watch. 'When the time is ripe, I shall of course go to Broadcasting House and speak to the nation.'

'When?'

'Not until morning, I think.' Sir Robert gave him a rallying smile. 'Everything's under control. The Army's in charge now, Mike, so you can relax.'

Mike wheeled sharply towards the curtained window. 'What's that?'

'I don't hear anything.'

'There's a light flashing outside.'

'That'll be one of my staff officers. I'm afraid the neighbours are in for a disturbed night.'

Parting the curtains, Mike peered out. 'Looks more like a police car,' he reported. 'And an ambulance. What do they want with a . . .'

His voice tailed off. He turned from the window. Still leaning against the door, the Field Marshal was eyeing him with an odd, unmilitary sympathy, not untouched by curiosity. 'I'm sorry, Mike,' he said earnestly.

'You two-faced bastard.'

'Now don't upset yourself. I've had assurances from the highest level about your family, so that's a weight off your mind, isn't it? All you need concentrate on is getting yourself fit. A few days of complete rest—'

'You gibbering jackass,' Mike said softly. 'I never imagined you could be as blinkered as all the rest.'

'Just take it easy, Mike. Everyone understands. Overstress is an insidious thing, it can crawl up unnoticed, wreak havoc before you know what's hit you. One thing about it, though, it responds to...' The door behind him shook under pressure. Standing clear, he let it open. 'Good evening, gentlemen. Thank you for coming along. Mr Willoughby's all ready for you.'

★   ★   ★

For the ninth time, someone came and shone a torch into his pupils. He spoke in a friendly tone to the nurse. 'What is it you're looking for? Maggots?'

A tall girl, broad in face and beam, she smiled dutifully. 'Doing nicely, Mr Willoughby. We might be sending you home before long.'

'I wonder you're ready to chance it.'

'Why? Not planning to set fire to the place, are you?'

'My plans are subtler than that.'

She began taking his pulse. 'You're a celebrity, you know. You'll have to watch your step.'

'What am I celebrated for?'

'Being off-song, for one thing.' The nurse produced and inserted a thermometer. 'There was a bit in one of the papers about you.'

'What am I suffering from?'

Her eyes widened. 'Overwork, of course. Isn't that what the doctor told you?'

'I don't remember much of what the doctor said. I'm sedated right?'

'That's to help you relax.'

'Okay, I'm relaxed. I couldn't get to that door if you pinned a million-quid note to it. What more do you want?'

'It's not a question of what I want.' Removing the thermometer, she examined it critically and put it away. 'Apart from the drowsiness, how do you feel in yourself?'

'Piecemeal.'

She looked at him uncertainly. 'We might have a surprise for you later.'

The room came and went. Now and then there was a muted rumble of trolley wheels outside; more occasionally, the soft thud of a door. Somebody brought him lunch. Steamed fish, jelly and ice-cream. He said to the orderly, 'What day is it?'

'Monday, sir.'

'I've been here . . . three nights?'

'That's it. Full board.'

'Can you do something for me? Find me a copy of yesterday's *Clarion*?'

'You're meant to be resting . . .'

'I only want to glance at it.'

'I'll see what I can do.'

Half an hour later the orderly returned with the edition. 'You're not to read more than ten minutes at a stretch, understood?'

'That's all right. It won't take me that long.'

He studied the front page for three minutes before dropping the newspaper to the floor.

In mid-afternoon the broad-featured nurse put part of herself around the door. 'Awake, Mr Willoughby? How are your paternal feelings at the moment?'

'Just send them in,' he said quietly.

Caroline, the brasher of the pair, entered first with doubt in her eyes. Alison hovered at the door, examining from a distance. With an effort he extended both arms.

'Well, you two. I thought you were never coming. Don't I get a large kiss on each cheek?'

Caroline darted. The bright warmth of her face sent a shiver of conflicting emotions through him. From the other side, Alison homed in to hug him cautiously, as if being allowed to handle the best china. Caroline murmured into his left ear.

'What, darling?'

She wriggled. 'Mummy said you might be coming home soon.'

'Mummy did? I hope Mummy's right. Is she here?'

'In the corridor. She told us to come in first.'

'And how are you all?'

'Jimmy cut his face again,' announced Alison.

'Poor old James. He'll be a walking surgery. Have you been staying with Auntie Becky?'

'No,' Caroline said blankly. 'We've been at home.'

'The whole time?'

'Yes, Daddy, of couse we have. It's not until

the sixteenth we go to Florida. Will you be better by then?'

'I'm better now. Why doesn't one of you go and fetch Mummy?'

'I'll go!' Alison scampered for the door.

Caroline fingered the top button of Mike's pyjamas. 'Mummy says you've been over ... overdoing it. She says she's not surprised you were ill.'

'When did Mummy say this? When she got back?'

'Back from where?

'Hasn't she been away?'

Caroline looked at him frowningly. 'You're the one who's been away.'

'And I hope it's done you some good,' said Lyn, entering behind Alison to sit next to Caroline on the bed. Although pale, she was looking at her best in a cool cream dress, her hair disarranged in the way that suited her. She studied him closely. 'You're looking better,' she added, with faint emphasis upon the middle word. 'Girls not exhausting you?'

'Only when they're not here.' He returned her gaze with a searching one of his own. 'So, I was pushing things too far?'

'I seem to recall warning you six months ago. You wouldn't have it.'

'All too much for the elderly gentleman. Well, he's submitting now, as you see. The model patient. How's life treated you just

211

lately?'

She shrugged with an indifference that betokened the depth of her concern. 'Fine, apart from a collapsed husband. What do you think about the sixteenth?'

'What about it?'

'Will you feel up to the trip? If necessary, we can—'

'I expect you're all anxious to get away. What was it last week?' he enquired. 'A trial run?'

'What?'

'Your few nights away from home. I thought maybe you were just testing how it felt.'

A shadow of alarm crossed her face. 'I've not been away,' she replied lightly. 'Did someone tell you I had?'

'Perhaps I misheard. You weren't out any night last week?'

'You're a fine one to ask a thing like that. Now listen, Mike. I've just had a word with the sister. According to her, the doctor says there's no reason why you shouldn't come home tomorrow, provided you agree to take it quietly and *relax*. You're not to concern yourself with anything.'

'Me? Concern myself?'

She eyed him dubiously. 'I'm not sure it's such a good idea. There's less temptation here to . . .' She stopped, wrinkling her nose at the bed-cover. 'I've just remembered. Mother said she rang last Thursday evening and you told her the girls were staying the night with someone and I was out on the town, or something. That must have been the start of your ... breakdown. The twins and I were all at home that evening, same as any other time.'

'Then why did I take the call?'

'She must have phoned you at the office. You know how absent-minded she gets.'

He nodded slowly, watching her face. 'That's probably it.'

'Though what made you think we were all having a night out...' Lyn broke off. 'It's really not important. What matters is getting you fit for the airport a few days from now. What do you think? Would you sooner come home?'

'I'll be guided by medical opinion. I'm in the hands of the experts, after all. They obviously know best.'

'Mike, do you feel all right?'

'Improving by the minute. Why?'

'You're being awfully amenable. It's not like you.'

'Post-anæsthetic compliance. It'll wear off.'

'You've not been under anæsthetic, and anyway there's no such thing.' She leaned forward to kiss him. 'The girls and I would like you home. What do you say? Can you put up with us?'

CHAPTER SEVENTEEN

Explosive giggles came at intervals from the carpet by the sliding doors. With some hilarity, the twins were playing Snap. From the hall, Lyn's voice drifted in semi-intelligible expostulatory bursts. Staring idly at the clue to Thirteen Down, Mike allowed the ballpen in his fingers to trace a senseless design on the *Custodian*'s eastern border. Slipping free, the ballpen dropped to the floor with a clatter.

Caroline looked across. 'Like a game, Daddy?'

'In a minute, darling.' Retrieving the pen, which was the one given to him by Dulcie, he placed it on a nearby coffee-table. Outside, Lyn's voice soared a little.

'I still don't understand it. Mike wasn't here. And I'm sure I've never uttered a word about seeing an old friend in London. I've lost touch with most of them. You're positive it was Mike you were talking to?'

An interval. 'Well, have we got the right evening? Thursday? It's beyond me. Why didn't I hear the phone? I could have met you on Friday morning, I wasn't doing anything. It's a complete mystery... What? Oh, he's having to rest, that's all. According to the doctor...'

Her voice dipped to near-inaudibility.

214

Picking up the ballpen, Mike drew a Grecian urn in the margin, hatching finely to accentuate its curves. When Lyn eventually re-entered the room he glanced up with a cheerful grin.

'Got things sorted out with the scatty parent?'

'Not really.' She sounded abstracted. Collecting the empty coffee cups and the girls' fruit juice tumblers, she paused on her way back to the door. 'She insists she spoke to you, here, early on Thursday evening last week. She seems quite definite about it.'

'Funny we should both be under the same illusion.'

'But you weren't here. And I was.' A tumbler fell to the carpet. 'Damn,' she said, grabbing it up. 'She *must* have rung you at the office, and got confused.'

Mike added flowers to the Grecian urn.

★   ★   ★

'I thought you had orders to rest.'

'I'm resting. The telephone seat's very comfortable and I've a Scotch at my right elbow. Just calling to thank you, George, a little belatedly, for giving my modest piece such prominence and resisting the urge to knock it about.'

'Think nothing of it.' Restraint had Pershaw's vocal delivery in a steel clamp. 'Glad to oblige.'

'I think that wraps it up.'

215

'Seems to. How are you feeling, Mike?'

'Slightly off-beam. Nothing a good holiday won't remedy.'

'Take as long as you need. You've earned a rest.'

'No particular date you want me back?'

'Suit yourself entirely. Things are quiet just now. You'll have to excuse me, Mike, I'm wanted on the intercom. Take it easy, okay?'

'I'll do that. Thanks, George. Nice to hear a friendly voice.'

Lyn emerged from the kitchen. 'What did he have to say?' she asked casually.

'Wished us a good holiday. I'm going out for half an hour.'

'Don't overdo it.'

'I'm not...' He stifled the retort. 'I can still manage a mile or two,' he said, more gently, and kissed her before leaving the house.

The local shopping precinct had a newsagent's, from which he bought the late edition of the evening paper, and a coffee-house, where he took it to read. Ordering lemon tea, he enquired after the health and family of Mrs Mortimer, who ran the place, and learned that her eldest daughter had just gained entrance to university. 'That's my bit of good news,' she said, bringing him a plate of biscuits. 'Things all right with you now, Mr Willoughby? On the mend, are you?'

'I'm fine. Don't believe all you read.'

She sniffed. 'Load of nonsense, most of it. I wouldn't take too much notice of anything they say.' She nodded at his evening paper. 'Especially that lot.' She gave him a friendly, commiserating look and went off to serve another customer. The customer was Miss Miriam Thrace, with whom Mike and Lyn were slightly acquainted. She was a leading activist on the Right-wing political scene in the district. He gave her a wave across the tables.

She responded with the merest semblance of a nod before turning a little in her chair to present him with her left shoulder. Evidently she wasn't feeling chatty. Mike picked up the newspaper. The lead story concerned the Government's rout of the Opposition over defence expenditure. Boxed to one side was an editorial pronouncement: *Those Wild Rumours ... What the Echo says. See page 18*. He turned the sheets.

Headed *Storm in a Coronet*, the Echo's leader column kicked off:

Lord Manninge's retraction yesterday of his somewhat vague allegations against an even vaguer caucus of political associates will have done no harm to his deserved reputation for objectivity and fair-mindedness.

Concerned as Lord Manninge undoubtedly was over unconfirmed reports relating to the recent tragic death of his son-in-law, Mr Patrick Godimer, there can be no justification for the fostering of wild and ludicrous rumours. His lordship's acknowledgement of this fact, in the shape of yesterday's unreserved statement amounted to a handsome admission that both he and his daughter, Lady Tessa Godimer, had clearly been over-hasty in their reaction to what must be described as non-events . . .

'Anything more you want, Mr Willoughby?'

'No thank you, Mrs Mortimer. I'm supposed to be on a diet. I'm not in the best of shape, they tell me.'

'Shame. The rock cakes are extra spicy today. Never mind—in another week or two, perhaps.'

'Let's hope so.' He dredged a thin smile to exchange for her plump one, rose, abandoned the newspaper and walked out of the coffee-house without a further glance at Miriam Thrace's jutting left shoulderblade. Thirty yards along the precinct stood a call-box. A woman was talking inside: he waited patiently, stationing himself a short way off to avoid any hint of harassment. When finally he gained admittance he found his mind a blank and was forced to consult Directory Enquiries for the *Echo*'s number. Having dialled and reached the switchboard, he asked for the news desk.

'Wilf Corrigan there? Charles Porter, then. Charlie? Mike—Mike Willoughby. I know you're busy so I'll keep it short. Would you be interested in a follow-up to the Godimer/

Manninge story? I can offer—'

'Mike, how are you?' The warmth of the enquiry all but melted the line. 'Hear you're taking a well-earned break, you pampered devil. Off to the Florida beaches soon, is that right?'

'Never mind that. Can you use a story?'

'We can always use a story. Tell you what: why don't you give us another call when you get back from the States? By that time—'

'I've read the editorials. There's another side to it, Charlie.'

'Sure there is. We'll be hearing about it from the *Clarion*?'

'I'm offering it to you.'

'Well ... we appreciate it, Mike. We really do. Thanks for thinking of us. Tell you what: suppose I switch you over to a copytaker and then we can read for ourselves what it is you're—'

'Tell you what, Charlie,' said Mike. 'Why don't you go and get yourself stewed in your own foundry?'

He hung up.

★　　★　　★

After the evening meal he stared unblinkingly at a comedy show on the TV. The spasmodic mirth of the twins, side by side on the floor with their backs to the sofa, came remotely to his ears like the swish of wavelets on a hidden strand. Lyn's attention was with a sock she was sewing.

When his gaze moved from the screen to her bent head she looked up, instantly aware.

He said, 'There's something I'd like you to do.'

A canned outburst from the set made her wince, leave her chair to occupy the one next to his. 'What is it?'

'Call your mother. Ask her if you and the girls can go over and stay the night.'

'Now? Tonight? That's absurd, Mike. We couldn't possibly—'

'She'll have you, won't she?'

'I dare say she'd jump at the idea. But if you think I'm going to travel miles with the girls at this time of day . . .' She paused, chewing her lip. More quietly she added, 'Why, Mike? Are we getting on your nerves?'

'It's not that.'

'You just need some peace and quiet?'

'I need to know the three of you are somewhere secure for the next twelve hours, at least.'

She stared blindly at the screen. The churning of her thoughts was almost a tangible vibration in his own head.

'Despite what the papers say,' he said presently, 'I'm not yet out of my mind. Do you believe that?'

'You don't have to ask,' she said, almost immediately.

'Remember the conversation you had with

your mother this morning?'

'I've done nothing but think about it.'

Mike glanced at the twins, who were engrossed in the on-screen gymnastics. 'There's a reason for the apparent inconsistency. Do you believe *that*?'

She gestured helplessly. 'It's hard for me to—'

'Do I sound incoherent?'

Watching him, she shook her head.

'Then will you do this for me? Just for tonight?'

She lifted a pair of resigned shoulders. 'You'll be all right, here by yourself?'

He smiled faintly. 'I shan't be here. But you're not to worry—you mustn't imagine things. I have to go and interview somebody, that's all. It'll be very boring and it probably won't take me anywhere, but I have to give it a try. Right? Now don't argue, love, because you'll be wasting your time. Please go and ring your mother.'

With a glance at the twins, Lyn rose silently and went out to the hall.

*   *   *

After telephoning to confirm that they had arrived and were settled in, Mike left the house and opened the garage door.

His jacket lay on the front passenger seat of the Cortina, where he had left it on his return from the shopping precinct: Putting it on, he

221

checked on the supply of ballpens clipped to the breast pocket: satisfied, he started the car and reversed into the road. Braking at the kerbside, he lowered the window and spoke to the empty pavement.

'I won't be long,' he said. 'Better get the kids to bed, love, they're looking sleepy.'

He drove the Cortina away.

CHAPTER EIGHTEEN

'Michael—what a surprise! Come on inside.'

'If I've chosen a bad time, say so. It's nothing that can't wait.'

'There's only this boring thrash at the Holbeam Gallery to launch somebody's new show, and I needn't be there for hours. Drink? You look at melting-point.'

'It's turned muggy out.' He followed Dulcie through to a brightly papered living-room strewn with white leather chairs of a sensual obesity. 'A bit thundery. I left my jacket in the car.'

'So I see.' She threw him a sisterly glance from the drinks trolley. 'Not often M.W. shows himself in disarray.' Bringing him a long glass of a fizzing compound infested with ice chunks, she collapsed gracefully into the plump embrace of one of the chairs and raised her own. 'Here's

222

to scandal. No. Here's to a nice, uncomplicated chat outside office hours.'

'Good to know that someone's still talking to me.'

She came and sat next to him. 'What do you take me for? I felt so sorry, Michael, when I heard you . . . weren't well. Everyone did.'

'I wasn't too delighted myself. Came at the wrong time, just when . . . However, one can't fly in the face of medical advice. Glad I caught you in, Dulcie. I'd have phoned earlier, but you know how it is. One gets these sudden impulses.'

'Impulsiveness,' she said demurely, 'can be stimulating. Just the same, you don't fool me, you know. You didn't come here to weep on my shoulder, Michael, that's not your style. You came with a purpose. Still hankering after that joint story of ours?'

'I was hoping,' he admitted, 'you might be able to help. Right now, I need all the support I can get.'

She resettled herself in a half-resigned but businesslike manner. 'I should have known it had nothing to do with my personal magnetism. Shoot.'

'Not here, if you don't mind. Come out for a drive.'

She looked at him in surprise. 'Are you serious?'

'I think better,' he explained, 'when I have

something to do with my hands and feet. Apart from which, there's something I want to show you.'

'An invitation like that, no virginal girl could possibly resist. As long as you'll drop me off at the gallery later.'

Outside, the sky was a piecrust trapping the baked air of the city. Moisture rose to the skin at the least movement. With the ventilation set to maximum, Mike took the Cortina out of the cobbled mews and into Eaton Square before heading west.

'On an evening like this,' he observed, 'a car is the coolest place. How do you manage it, Dulcie?'

'Manage what?'

'To look permanently fresh. Don't lady columnists have sweat-glands?'

She gave him a prim look. 'I must say, Michael, you don't *sound* like a convalescent. Are you quite sure this whole thing isn't some kind of red herring?'

He frowned over the wheel. 'Come again?'

'This malady of yours. It's not a plot you've hatched with George Pershaw to disguise the fact that you're still investigating?'

'Now there's a thought,' he said with amusement. 'I wish it were true. The fact is, I'm left with no base for further investigation. Everyone knows that.'

'It's a terrible shame.'

'Humiliation might be nearer the mark.' He tossed her a quick glance. 'Tell me something, Dulcie. Do you believe all the things that have been said about me?'

'Having now spoken to you again, I take leave to doubt some of them. On the other hand, Michael . . .' A note of earnestness stole into her voice. 'I do think there comes a time when that medical advice you were talking about shouldn't be ignored. You've pushed yourself, haven't you, for quite a while? A matter of years. No engine can last at top revs for ever.'

He was silent for a moment while turning the car south towards Chelsea. 'Maybe not. But without oil and usage it'll seize up. I said I wanted your help, Dulcie. That stands. I'd like to try something on you. Mind if I go ahead?'

'Be gentle, sir, quoth the maiden. I'm all ears.'

With automatic movements he threaded the Cortina through the evening traffic. 'You know what I've been chasing,' he said presently. 'If I were sitting down now to write a preliminary story, it might include the following queries. One: who was so eager to put me out of the running from the start? And two: whoever it was, how were they so successful? How come that whatever I did, wherever I went, somebody was always a jump ahead of me?'

She looked at him seriously. 'Go on.'

'Twice I was nearly killed. Not only that: two

225

innocent people died after I'd had contact with them. I think I know why. What I'd like to know is how.'

'You were being followed,' she suggested.

'That's the obvious explanation, but it falls short. My every action seemed to be monitored. It was uncanny. How do you account for that?'

'I can't. Social gossip is my line, not clairvoyance.'

'Well, as a social writer, haven't you ever wished you could overhear all kinds of juicy morsels normally unavailable to you?'

She gave a throaty chuckle. 'Haven't we all? Michael, before you go any further I want to start making some notes. It sometimes helps. Can I borrow a pen?'

'You'll find several in my jacket. Notepad too.'

Hauling it from the rear seat, she unclipped a ballpen from the breast pocket, transferred it to her left hand while searching for the pad. 'Men's pockets,' she complained. 'Talk about women's handbags... I have it. Proceed with your thesis.'

'You won't do much with that one, Dulcie.'

'What?'

'The pen you've chosen. It's a bad writer. The first one you picked out was much better— why did you chuck it away?'

Her pencilled eyebrows drew closer together. 'Whatever do you mean?'

226

'I mean it was a nice try, Dulcie, but you really needn't have bothered. The pen you've just dropped out of the window cost me three quid in a stationer's this afternoon, but in the circumstances I can afford to waste that kind of money.'

'You're talking very oddly, Michael. Are you feeling well?'

'What I'm feeling is talkative. Let me rattle on for a bit. That pen you've just got rid of: you thought, didn't you, it was the one you lent me last week? It wasn't. That one is in my desk drawer at the office: I called in there to dump it on my way to you.'

'How intersting. We seem to have slipped away from the subject.'

'On the contrary. Why, you're probably asking yourself, did I take the trouble to buy myself a replica of a ballpen you lent me, and leave the original somewhere else? Or could I be wrong? Could you perhaps be asking yourself just how much else I know?'

'I'm starting to ask myself if I should jump out here and call a cab.'

'Try if you like.'

Her wrench at the door handle produced no result. Mike gave her a paternal smile.'

'Before leaving,' he murmured, 'I took the precaution of fixing the lock. It only opens from the outside.'

'I'm having serious second thoughts,

227

Michael, about your condition.'

'Please don't worry about me. Now that I know I've been carrying a close-range micro-transmitter under my chin for the past eight days, you can't imagine how great I feel.'

He watched her reach through the open window and tug at the outer handle. 'You need the door key,' he informed her. 'Sorry I didn't bring my spare. Had a feeling we shouldn't be needing it.'

'I demand that you stop and let me out.'

'Without hearing the rest? That does surprise me a little. On past form, I'd have thought you'd want to learn as much as possible.' He changed lanes to sprint for a junction. 'I have to hand it to you, Dulcie. The idea was as simple as it was brilliant. All part of KGB training?'

'Now you really are fantasizing.'

'Hypothesizing. There's more to it than a mere awareness that your job with the *Clarion* gives you the perfect cover. There's also the evidence on file.'

'Evidence of what?'

'Last week, quite by chance, I stumbled on an old picture in the course of some research in the Morgue. It showed a group of politicians, among them our Premier, under enthusiastic bombardment from a mob of Left-wingers some years ago. Some of the faces could be seen quite plainly.'

'Thrilling.'

'Well, I *was* thrilled, I have to admit, when I recognized one of them. It was under a beret, but there was no mistaking it as yours, Dulcie.'

'My radical past catching up with me.'

'Could that have been when you were spotted and recruited, I wonder?'

She said carelessly, 'At one time I did hold fairly extreme views. Rebellion against a stuffy land-owning dad. I did join an activist group for a while. It's no crime.'

'Indeed not. Many would applaud your stand against a party leader of such a remarkably far-Right calibre.'

'I still think his policies stink.'

'Which ones? Those that he professes, or the real job-lot?'

'I've no idea what you mean.'

'In that case, let's return to matters of more immediate concern. Those bids on my life I was complaining about. I've been giving them some thought. Pretty clumsy, wasn't it, the reasoning behind them? Murder the guy who's investigating, and nobody else will smell a rat? Wonder-Boy Ralph would never have authorized such attempts. He at least had the brains to realize that something subtler was called for. So could it be, I ask myself, that his paymasters simply took matters into their own hands and went their separate ways about eliminating me?'

'Persecution complex, it's called.'

'Alf Barnard and Dave Philcox must have felt persecuted, too. If they had time to feel anything.'

'How could their deaths have been anything but accidental? They knew very little that might have been dangerous. They were just village people who noticed slightly more than the rest of the inhabitants.'

The Cortina was now clear of the Chelsea tangle, speeding east along the Embankment. Mike had time to transfer his gaze from the road to her.

'You seem astoundingly well-informed, Dulcie. I've never spoken to you about either of them. How come you're so thoroughly versed in the detail?'

She turned away to stare at the passing buildings. 'Where are we going?' she demanded.

Mike grinned. 'Always answer one question with another. Classic ploy when the going gets heavy. I thought maybe we'd pay some friends of mine a visit—there's usually a welcome. Oh, and Dulcie. I wouldn't try anything on the way. That really might tend to confirm my worst impressions.'

★　　　★　　　★

Although his eyes were bright, Sergei's face was unsmiling. He spoke softly.

230

'This is the lady, Mikail? The one you said you might be bringing to see us.'

'I hope it's not causing you any trouble, Sergei.'

'She'll cause us no trouble.'

'I'd like her looked after for a while. Well looked after.'

'She shall have a taste of traditional Ukrainian hospitality. What do you say, Anna?'

'It will be a pleasure.'

Mike released Dulcie into the centre of the room. She stood rubbing her arm. 'I was brought here,' she announced, 'against my will. I've reason to believe that this man is dangerously unbalanced. Will you please either allow me to leave or let me telephone the police?'

Sergei gave her a thoughtful survey. 'No,' he said briefly. 'That might not be in the best interests of anybody. Anna, will you keep our guest company for a moment?'

Stationing herself at Dulcie's side, his wife turned a radiant smile in Mike's direction. 'It's no trouble at all,' she reiterated. 'Good night, Mikail, and good luck.'

'Anna is highly efficient,' Sergei said on the landing.

'I know you both are. Otherwise I wouldn't have asked. Can you keep her here, Sergei, incommunicado, for at least the next twenty-four hours?'

'It's no problem. Is she KGB?'

'Almost certainly, though I can't prove it. What I do know is, she can ruin my plans if she's allowed contact with her control in the next day or so. Do I ask too much?'

'You don't ask enough,' the exile assured him. 'Go and do what you must, Mikail. The media are giving you a hard time, but there are still a few of us who have faith in you. Don't forget that.'

At the further end of Southwark Street, Mike found a usable call-box and dialled a number. Having spoken, he returned to the car and drove to the underground car park at Marble Arch.

CHAPTER NINETEEN

'Let's walk.'

Fifty yards down Park Lane, the tall white-jacketed man with an easy stride said, 'I shouldn't be seen with you, Mike. Contact with screwy newsmen is strictly frowned upon. This is for old times's sake, okay? We've had a productive relationship in the past. You've slipped us a few useful tips: we've helped you a little, I hope. We don't forget all that. But what's this we've been reading and hearing about you? Did you crack up?'

'Do I look or sound like it?'

'You're looking kind of bushed.' The other's

drawl was as unhurried as his gait. 'Aside from that, I wouldn't want to jump to conclusions.' He paused. 'These rumours concerning your family, how'd they get around?'

'They originated from me.'

'Then what—'

'Only they're not rumours. They happen to be fact. My wife and children were abducted to put pressure on me. Then they were returned.'

'You can't expect—'

'But not without precautions, Joe.'

The other looked at him. 'What's that supposed to mean?'

'Their minds had been doctored. I'm serious. No, I can't prove it, but do I need to? If what I'm saying is right, the best practitioners were available and they had a few days to work in. With all the updated techniques, that's time enough, isn't it? Dope, hypnosis . . . How long does it take to wipe out memory? Not long, given the resources. Remember the Malakov Case?'

'Sure, but they had a month to work on him.'

'Yes, and they had a lifetime's conditioning to eradicate. In the case of my family, it was a relatively simple matter of suggesting, quite reasonably, that they'd spent those few days at home in the usual way instead of being transported and confined elsewhere, which is what actually happened.'

'An innocent woman and a couple of kids?'

'Naivety doesn't suit you, Joe. You know as well as I do, if the stakes are high enough, minor considerations of that sort don't apply. A few mild doses of a pentathol-derivative, a day or two of gentle but insistent brainwashing ... what does that amount to, set against the matter in hand?'

'Whatever that is. You haven't told me yet.' The man whom he knew as Joe took a kick at a pebble on the pavement as he walked. 'I'll give you the method: no special problems there. Nice clean job, reliable, no after-traces to speak of. Now convince me it was worth someone's while to go to all that trouble with the family of a working journalist.'

'I'll try to convince you in a minute. First I want you to be clear on the basic facts, which are that by the time Lyn and the girls had been taken home again the entire episode of their absence had been cleaned out of their minds, clinically and effectively, by experts; with the result that my subsequent account of their disappearance sounded like nonsense. It was done to discredit me, and it worked like a charm. I'm a joke-figure. Even my news editor thinks I'm nuts.'

'Okay, you've been set up. Who's responsible?'

'Whitehall.'

'You're saying, there's an official campaign to—'

'*Official* is too comprehensive. I'm coming to that, but just let me fill you in. Because of what's happened, nothing I say now is treated seriously. Everyone believes I've suffered a mental breakdown. My own chief talks to me like a Dutch uncle, the inference being that I'll write another column over his dead body. It's the same all along the line. The other night, I asked a colleague to fix a meeting for me with the Home Secretary. Next thing I know, the cops are surrounding the rendezvous. By sheer chance—'

'Our assessment of Puttenham is hundred and ten per cent.'

'As it happens, mine is too. I accept that he acted in good faith, because like everyone else he believes my activities are a threat to internal security. Likewise the military. When in desperation I went to the top brass, I was humoured for an hour while the authorities were called to take me away. The high-ranking officer I spoke to is no traitor, Joe. He's a loyal soldier. He honestly believed he was acting in the nation's best interests. They all believe it.'

'You don't feel,' the other said mildly, 'there's a faint possibility they might just all be right?'

'I can understand the general attitude,' Mike said after a few moments. 'When the truth is unthinkable, naturally it doesn't occur to anyone to give it house-room.'

'So what makes you think the CIA will be any different?'

Mike gazed across the dim mystery of Hyde Park. 'Two things. You constitute a more dispassionate eye: less emotionally involved, so to speak. Also you present the other country that's most vitally affected. You're my last throw.'

'Okay. Try me. What's the incredible truth?'

'First, I'll give you the lie. The story goes that Pat Godimer was rubbed out because he planned to pass the secrets of Rainblast to Moscow.'

Joe's voice didn't change. 'New to us. Where did that one originate?'

'From an unimpeachable source. The Prime Minister himself.'

'Well, he should know.'

'Certainly he does. He knows the real truth: that Godimer was a potential obstacle to just such a plan.'

Joe halted in mid-stride. 'Now wait a bit. On that basis—'

'I'm telling you. Our volubly Right-wing Premier himself is the far-Left menace. He's a phoney, Joe. He was got at, years ago, way back at university or maybe even before. Recognized as Number Ten material, given the Rightist image, told to cultivate it at every turn. It took him twenty-five years, thirty, you name the period, but he made it. In addition to power, he now has the total confidence of virtually everyone in the West who counts ... and he's under direct control from the Kremlin. I can't prove it but I know it. I'm in an impossible position.'

The CIA man had been listening in a half-trance. Now he went and leaned on a railing, staring into the park as if half-expecting to witness the gambolling of nymphs and fauns. 'Do I take you seriously or don't I?'

'See what I mean?'

After half a minute's deliberation Joe twisted slowly, rested both elbows on the railing, waited for an entwined couple to pass beyond earshot. 'If Godimer stood in the way, why did Langholme have him at Defence in the first place?

'Isn't it obvious? He had to, so as to convince Washington that his own commitment to a get-tough policy towards Moscow was as firm as he made out. Godimer was already well established as a hawk. He was a reassurance to the Pentagon. Would they have contemplated selling us Rainblast otherwise?'

'But—'

'Once the deal was close to agreement, Godimer had served his purpose and was expendable. Before the secrets of the system were actually passed to us, Langholme needed someone compliant in his place at Defence.'

'Mel Beattock?'

'Exactly. I've no proof in his case, either, but I think he's a long-term mole with Langholme. He was at Coverdale around the same time ... he could even have been the one who conveyed the first overtures from Moscow. And why, suddenly, has he now been given the Defence portfolio? Previously his career seemed to be petering out. It's as if he was being held in reserve.'

'You're reading an awful lot, Mike, into precious little. Why couldn't Langholme have simply fired Godimer?'

'That might have signalled a policy switch to Washington. They could have got cold feet and cancelled the deal.'

'The fact of his being killed could have had the same effect.'

'Has it?'

Joe was silent. Mike added, 'If I'm any judge, your Government thinks the same as most of Britain: it accepts Godimer's death as a pure accident, as it was meant to. Now, it's prepared to take his replacement on trust and finalize the Rainblast negotiations. Unless you know anything to the contrary?'

'Dammit, Mike,' Joe protested. 'We've heard no whispers. Surely your own security people—'

'With the possible exception of a planted pathologist and one or two others, KGB agents did the actual dirty work on Langholme's

238

behalf, and as we all know they can be quite discreet. As for any subsidiary operations, they were carried out by the EPS ... and the EPS, you may recall, is very much Langholme's own baby. He had it set up ostensibly for special security purposes, and I'm willing to bet its fifty-odd membership was hand-picked by the Kremlin.'

'Then how—'

'Luckily for me, its ranks have either been penetrated by a genuine Right-wing agent or at least one of its number is starting to have serious qualms about its activities. Whatever the case, I owe my freedom to that individual.'

By tacit consent they started walking again. Mike watched the traffic, letting the CIA man think things through. A police car passed at speed in the outer lane, its roof-lamp flashing; he remained tense until it was out of sight. The sultriness of the evening was regenerating the throb inside his head.

'You say you've no proof,' Joe murmured.

'All the proof I need lies in what happened to me and my family. I *know* what's been going on.'

'Sure you're not letting it cloud your judgement?'

'You think I imagined it?'

'Don't get me wrong, Mike. Your credentials have always been good with us. The best. But facts are still facts. The way I see it, there's this very special cross-Atlantic relationship, a thing of long standing based on mutual respect and collaboration: you don't set out to question an established partnership, from which proven benefits have flowed, without first—'

'I'm not blind to the arguments, Joe. It's things like this that people like you are supposed to be in business to dispose of.'

'Sure, but even the CIA doesn't leap in with both feet without looking.'

'I'm not asking it to. I'm asking it to approach this with an open mind.' Mike stopped again. 'Only I get the feeling I'm pitching my request too high. For someone who imagines people are trying to kill him and kidnap his family, it's a lot to expect. Here he is, after all. Comic old M.W. of the *Clarion*, still shambling around, still surrounded by his loved ones. Nothing's happened to him yet: ergo, it must be delusion. Langholme did a good job, didn't he, Joe?'

The CIA man clapped his shoulder. 'Take it easy, Mike. Right now you're too upset to see things straight. Leave it with me, okay? Meantime, I suggest you go home and rest up.'

★   ★   ★

One of the coffee-shops in Shepherd Market was encircled by outside tables. Most were taken, but a vacancy remained at the perimeter, half-concealed by a potted shrub, and Mike claimed it. Seated in a huddle, with untasted coffee festering in the cup at his elbow, he observed without registration the perambulations of the tourists and the purposeful progress of the locals, bound for elsewhere. Fragments of dialogue reached him from other tables.

'... take in a disco later ...' 'She wasn't too pleased, but as I told her, you can't ...' '... defiance of natural law ...'

A middle-aged man and his older wife, or young aunt, rose and abandoned the adjoining table, leaving a copy of the evening paper's final edition on one of the seats. Reaching across, Mike harvested the catch.

The page one story was an analysis by the Defence Correspondent of the financial implications of the mooted Rainblast deal. Under a sub-heading, *No Split—And That's Official*, James Holt of the political staff laid stress on the Cabinet's surface unity on the issue.

Following the adjournment for the Summer Recess—delayed by the extension of the Session to allow for debates on a number of important aspects of Government policy—the Premier later tonight will attend a meeting of some of his own Backbenchers to allay their misgivings about the cost of Rainblast over the next few years. He then plans to spend the weekend at Chequers, putting the final touches to the ...

Mike consulted his watch. Returning the newspaper to the seat, he rose and walked off towards Piccadilly, covering some distance before an available taxi came along. 'Westminster,' he told the driver.

*   *   *

One of the two policemen on duty at the western entrance offered Mike a contrained greeting. 'Long while, Mr Willoughby. How's life treating you?'

'Variable, thanks. Hoped someone like yourself might be here, Walter. All right if I step inside for half an hour?'

The two officers exchanged glances. 'Far as I'm personally, concerned, Mr Willoughby, you know there'd be no objection. It's the red tape that's the problem. Passholders only ... the usual caper.'

'Come on, Walt. You're not dealing with some faceless anarchist from the *Workers' Chronicle.*'

Embarrassment crept into the policeman's stance. 'Sorry, Mr Willoughby. I'd personally be happy to let you through, but my hands are tied. Geoff here'll bear me out.'

Mike turned to Geoff. 'I wouldn't want anyone disregarding orders. Just interpreting them flexibly. Up until quite recently I was fully accredited, and I'm still—'

'We've got our instructions, sir,' Geoff said

stolidly.

Walter was looking unhappy. 'Mr Willoughby *was* a passholder for a good long while . . .'

His colleague gave him a slight shake of the head.

Mike said pleasantly, 'I see you've been reading the papers.'

'Rules are quite clear, sir. No admittance without a pass.'

There was a brief silence.

'Tell you what,' said Walter. 'You did say half an hour, Mr Willoughby?'

'If that. I just want a quick word with someone.'

'I'll step along with you.' He consulted his colleague. 'Fair enough? If I keep Mr Willoughby company while he's inside, that should cover it. I'll send Frank out to join you.'

The jaw of his fellow-officer took a dive, but sound failed to emerge. While he was still searching for words, Walter brandished Mike through and tailed him to an open door which gave access to an interior corridor. They fell into step, their heels creating echoes.

'Very good of you, Walter. Hope I'm not endangering your promotion.'

The policeman gave a thin smile. 'It's managed to avoid me up to now. Why should next year be any different?'

'Sorry to hear that. You must find it difficult,

making ends meet.'

'It's a struggle,' Walter replied carelessly. 'But then I'm no different from anyone else.'

'That's a matter of opinion.' At a turn in the corridor, Mike came to a halt and looked swiftly both ways before extracting his wallet. 'You know how the *Clarion* and I have always appreciated your co-operation,' he remarked, stuffing some notes into the other's tunic pocket.

'Always happy to oblige, Mr Willoughby. I think you know your way from here. When you come back, I'll be waiting at the end there to see you out.' Without alteration of expression he added, 'Geoff's a stickler for the formalities.'

'He'll go far.'

Walking on a short distance, Mike climbed a flight of stairs and continued along another corridor that led to a gallery housing a number of doors. On the way, he was passed by several uniformed officials, each of whom he wished a genial good evening. The third was known to him by sight. He paused.

'Has the PM arrived yet?'

'On his way up to the meeting, sir.'

'Usual room, I take it?'

'Same as always, Mr Willoughby. Most of 'em are there now.'

'Thank you.'

From the far end of the gallery appeared a trio of MPs, laughing uproariously at a shared joke.

At sight of Mike they fell silent. As they passed, one of them wished him a courteous good evening. Looking back, he saw them at the door to the meeting-room: the one who had greeted him was gazing his way with a small frown, saying something to his nearer companion.

Beyond the gallery, more stairs led down to a mezzanine vestibule. Leaning against a plinth supporting a bust of Disraeli, Mike waited.

Distantly, a door clashed. There was a brief hammering of feet. His muscles tautened, sagged again as the noise died. After an interval the sounds recurred, and this time the footfalls persisted, a medley of tiny explosions gaining progressively in volume. Quitting the plinth, Mike took up station in mid-vestibule, keeping his bandaged hand pocketed.

Into view from a turn in the staircase came the Prime Ministerial party, led by Langholme himself. Behind his left elbow, a short, tubby, bespectacled aide was hunting in a dispatch case, puffing as he climbed. None of the group was known to Mike. He stepped into their path. The Premier pulled up and the rest cannoned into each other like Disney buffoons before coming to a collective standstill behind him. Mike spoke clearly.

'A very good evening to you, Prime Minister. Can you spare a couple of minutes?'

Langholme shot out a restraining hand to the asthmatical aide, who was on the point of

245

bustling forward. 'All right, Philip. I'll deal with it. What is it you're after, Mr Willoughby?'

'I'd appreciate a quick word, if you'd be so kind.'

'What about?'

'A matter of national importance.'

'You're chasing an exclusive?'

'Prime Minister,' wheezed the aide, 'we're late for the meeting as it is . . .'

'I know. This needn't take long. I feel a little in Mr Willoughby's debt. Will you please go ahead, all of you, and explain that I've been unavoidably delayed and I'll be there shortly. Is there a room where Mr Willoughby and I can talk?'

'Facing you, Prime Minister, at the top of the stairs.' Swallowing his disapproval, the breathless Philip completed the ascent and threw open a door. 'You'll be undisturbed in here,' he said, eyeing Mike with disfavour.'

Politely, Langholme stood aside for Mike to go first. 'I'll be as quick as I can,' he informed the group outside, and closed the door in their faces.

The room was a midget office, furnished with a desk, three varnished wooden chairs of anti-vertebral design, and a filing cabinet against the blinded window. Flicking a switch, Langholme waited until the neon light flashed on and then adjusted the positions of two of the chairs. 'Do sit down, Mr Willoughby.'

Complying, Mike said reflectively, 'I seem to remember it got to first-name terms in the command post.'

'I'm afraid I don't follow.'

'Don't tell me you've forgotten already? That's deflating. I was starting to imagine I'd become quite important to you.'

Langholme lowered himself slowly on to the other chair. He sat in a posture of restrained authority, his head thrust forward a little in a way that suggested a charitable readiness to listen.

'You'll have to be more explicit. What's this about a command post?

'Since this is in confidence,' said Mike, 'we may as well ditch the language of diplomacy for the moment—what do you say?'

'I might know what to say, if I had the faintest idea what you're talking about.'

Mike gazed at him with a half-smile, and said nothing. The Prime Minister exhibited signs of restlessness. 'I really am a little pressed for time, you know. A matter of . . . national importance, I believe you said?'

'I admire your style, Langholme. There's nothing else I like about you, but you've the nerve of a baron. Stood you in good stead, hasn't it, over the years?'

'Would you mind coming immediately to the point?'

'Unhappily, nerve can develop into

arrogance. And arrogance, in turn, can make people overreach themselves: lead them to think they can play God. Manipulate others' lives. To say nothing of their deaths.'

Langholme glanced at his watch. 'I can give you one more minute, Mr Willoughby. If vague personal abuse is the only—'

'I've a proposition.' Mike waved him back to his chair. 'Shall I tell you what I think, Langholme? I think you see me as a sort of insect crawling in your hair. Each time you try to brush me off, I hop out of your way and land somewhere else. Irritating, isn't it? So, suppose I make it easy for you. You've done your best to wreck my livelihood. Here's the deal. In return for suitable compensation, I'll agree to leave the stage and retire into the wings . . . for good. How does that appeal to you?'

The Prime Minister studied him broodingly for a moment.

'The effect it has on me, Mr Willoughby, is to bemuse me utterly. I don't understand a word you're saying.'

'Then let me repeat what I was—'

'Please don't bother. I can't think we've anything relevant to say to each other. By the same token, the miniature tape-recorder you have concealed in your left pocket is being ludicrously misapplied. What is it, I wonder, you were hoping to pick up?'

Withdrawing his bandaged hand, Mike dealt

the pocket a thwack. 'As an old-fashioned journalist, Langholme, I've never much cared for electronics. In the past day or so I've gone off them even more. Mostly I rely on memory. This inconvenient cerebral filing system of mine that you'd love to send to the shredder. My offer remains open—why don't you think about it?'

'No need.' The Prime Minister stood up. 'This interview is finished. I'm sorry for you, Willoughby, but there's nothing I can do. Persecution mania is a medical problem, not a political one.'

'That depends.' Mike looked up smilingly. 'When I mentioned reliance on memory just now, I'm afraid I wasn't being entirely frank with you.'

Langholme became still. 'What do you mean?'

'I mean that unless we can reach an understanding, I shall feel at liberty to hand to the proper authorities a certain amount of documentary evidence in my possession.'

'Evidence?' the Prime Minister repeated quietly. 'Of what?'

'Among other things, a certain long-term relationship between here and Moscow. Stretching back—oh, twenty or thirty years, at the least. A historic record, you might say. The kind of thing that might widen a great many eyes in this country and elsewhere.'

'You've no such material. It doesn't exist.'

'But you've no idea what I'm referring to, Prime Minister. How can you deny the existence of "X" the Unknown?'

Breath emerged slowly from between Langholme's teeth. He stood motionless, staring at the wall.

A respectful double knock fell on the door. As though roused from a coma, the Premier turned and opened it. An agitated voice outside said, 'Prime Minister, we really ought to be—'

'All right, Philip. Mr Willoughby and I are almost through. Will you ask them to please be patient for a few more minutes? I'll be as speedy as I can.'

Gently, Langholme closed the door again. Walking across to the desk, the surface of which was empty, he sat on it with arms folded.

'Without prejudice,' he said, 'I'm prepared to hear an outline of what you have to say concerning this so-called evidence of an East-West . . . relationship. But as you know, I'm overdue at a meeting of my rank and file, so would you please hurry it up?'

'By all means,' agreed Mike. 'I'll make it very quick.' From his right-hand pocket he produced a notepad. 'First, I'd like you to take a look at this.'

Accepting the pad, Langholme groped for the reading glasses in his breast pocket. Mike was close at his side. He stationed his left hand immediately behind the Premier's neck: with his right fist he delivered a short, accurate blow to the point of the chin. Langholme's head jerked back against the restraining palm; his body slumped.

Mike lowered him carefully. When the Prime Minister was spreadeagled, face upwards, on the desktop, he placed a hand over the slack mouth and, with thumb and forefinger of the other, gently but firmly pinched the nostrils.

He allowed a full three minutes.

On removal of his hands, the face was faintly livid and the lips were blue. Traces of froth lurked at the mouth-corners. Mike felt for the pulse.

Once he was satisfied he made for the door. Letting himself out, he stared urgently around. The door of the meeting-room was in sight, and in its vicinity hovered the aide called Philip, glaring anxiously in his direction. Mike brandished an arm.

'Can you come quickly?' he called. 'I think the Prime Minister has been taken ill.'

The aide scuttled along. 'Get to a phone,' he said after a single glance. 'Call help.'

CHAPTER TWENTY

'While you're checking in the luggage,' said Lyn, 'the girls and I can be getting something to drink, right?'

'Fine. I'll join you in a little while.'

Having disposed of the suitcases, Mike went to the bookstall and bought a range of newspapers. Although the treatments varied, the content as disseminated by the Press agency was uniform. The *Record* had carried it verbatim, under his byline.

After two days of intensive questioning, I was allowed home yesterday to write this exclusive account of the sensational sudden death of the late Premier, Mr Ralph Langholme, in the course of an interview I was conducting with him at Westminster on Friday. Pathologists have now confirmed that a massive heart-attack . . .

Having read to the foot of the column, Mike turned to the editorial comment and permitted himself the faintest of smiles.

The Diplomatic Correspondent of the *Custodian*, Saul Posner, had been allowed to spread himself in a front-page examination of the crisis. The acting Premier, Henry

Puttenham, he wrote, had moved swiftly to establish his authority and rally the party, badly shaken by this second disaster within a fortnight. Already it was apparent that he intended to be more than a mere shadow of his predecessor, whom he had served loyally for so long. A Cabinet shake-up seemed imminent.

One key post likely to change hands again is that of Secretary of State for Defence, in which the performance to date of Mr Godimer's successor, Melvin Beattock, is understood to have caused Mr Puttenham and others in the party some concern. Other changes will follow, and they will not be confined to the Government ranks. It is reliably reported that a purge, modest in scale but far-reaching in consequence, has already begun in the upper reaches of the Civil Service. According to my information . . .

A bell-like voice rang in the terminal ceiling. 'Will Mr Willoughby, a passenger for Miami, please go to the airport information desk. Mr Willoughby to airport information.'

A young woman in staff uniform intercepted Mike as he approached. Her smile was brighter than the sun. 'Would you mind stepping this way, Mr Willoughby.'

'A *Sunday Clarion* reader, evidently.'

'Never miss your column, if I can help it. But they really ought to get a new photo of you.'

Leading the way to a rear door, she showed him into an office containing two men, one of whom rose at his entrance, said, 'You won't want me hovering,' flashed Mike a cryptic half-grin and went out. The other remained sprawled in a low-slung airport chair, scanning a typewritten and heavily-amended document while negligently conveying coffee ice-cream from a plastic tub to his capacious mouth with a matching plastic scoop. In mid-suck, he turned a hooded inspection on the new arrival.

'Greetings, Mike. What have you done with the family?'

'They went ahead to the buffet. I trust.'

'Relax, old boy.' The fleshy mouth puckered a little. 'The heat's off them now. All of you. That's official.'

'If it's as valid as most of the other official assurances I've been—'

'This one emanates from different sources. Entirely ... different ... sources,' said the other man with punctuated emphasis. He re-inserted the scoop into the tub, agitated it for a moment. 'No doubt you've been reading all the newspapers—as well as helping to write 'em. The purge accounts are substantially accurate.'

'Gory details to emerge in due course?'

'As the saying has it. If you want first strike—'

'Just now, I'd like to be first to the Florida beaches.'

'Your flight's been delayed,' the other said calmly. 'Which most fortuitously gives me time to carry out my instructions, which are, in essence, to transmit official appreciation plus cast-iron guarantees for the future.' A scoopful of ice-cream slithered down. 'You wouldn't care for one of these?'

'You're right, I wouldn't. Guarantees of what?'

A shrug. 'Diplomatic immunity, shall we call it? For want of a better phrase.'

'I wasn't worried about that.'

'There'd be a place for you, Mike, in the Service. An aptitude for the adroit falsehood is still the prime qualification. Whether you're in an anxiety state or not, I'm here to tell you that as far as H.M. Government is concerned you're off the hook. The Puttenham round-up is virtually complete...'

'He moves fast.'

'He'd very little choice. The Langholme inquest, on the other hand, will be delayed till you get back; but don't fret over that, either. It's all sewn up. The medical evidence will be meticulously worded. Anything you feel like uttering will be respectfully recorded for historians to distort. Happy?'

'Overjoyed.'

'Think of it,' advised the other on a rare note of solemnity, 'as nothing more than the crushing of a scorpion with the heel of your boot.'

'Oh, I do. All the time.'

'And try to remember you weren't acting in isolation, though at times it must have felt like it. Which reminds me. Somebody called Joe sends his profound gratitude and asks me to wish you a great little vacation on behalf of himself and fellow-directors of the New Jersey Export Corporation Inc. Also to say that, whatever the initial appearances to the contrary, neither he nor his associates make a practice of ignoring sound commercial advice, and he's sorry if he ever gave that impression.'

Mike nodded pensively. 'Tell him in return, if you would, they seem to have more than made up for it since. Mind if I go now? My family will be getting jumpy.'

Scrambling to his feet, the man interred the scoop in the tub and held out his free hand. Ignoring it, Mike moved to the door. The man pocketed the hand. 'If you ever want to consult me, you know where I am. You're staying on with the *Clarion*?'

'Not decided.'

'If you leave,' the other said chattily, 'it'll be the second major defection in a week. They've just lost Dulcie O'Farrell, I hear.'

'O'Farrell?'

'Her real name. Or one of her several false ones: we're not entirely sure which, but it's not important. I thought that might interest you. Seems she quit her London address a few days ago—just prior to the PM's death, in fact—and hasn't been seen since. I wonder what could have become of her?'

Their eyes met. Mike said, 'I can't imagine.'

'Oh well. You'll probably dig out the details eventually. Quite good at that, Mike, aren't you?'

'Some of us keep trying.'

★   ★   ★

'Who's going to fetch Daddy a coffee?'

Both girls pranced off to the service counter. Sitting down, Mike handed Lyn a selection of newsprint which she accepted resignedly. 'Our flight's held up, did you hear?'

'I heard.'

A headline at the foot of the *Custodian*'s front page had seized his attention. *Britain to lose Rainblast as US Thinks Again*. It was bylined 'By Our Westminster Staff.'

The acting Prime Minister, Mr Puttenham, is expected to announce during the recall of Parliament today that 'insuperable obstacles' have arisen to the planned deal whereby Britain was to have purchased the American Rainblast anti-missile system for its own defence. Although he is unlikely to specify the precise nature of the 'obstacles,' the gigantic cost of the system . . .

'We got you some biscuits too,' announced Caroline, returning breathlessly.

'That's kind. Suddenly I've quite an appetite.'

'Daddy.' Alison had advanced on his other flank. 'Can I have tennis coaching in Florida?'

'I don't see why not. Rackets are still excluded from the list of proscribed weapon imports, so far as I know.'

Lyn was eyeing him thoughtfully over the top of the *Record*. 'Nice story, love,' she said. 'When do you plan to tell the rest of it?'

He released a shattered shortcake from its Polythene tomb. 'What makes you think it's incomplete?'

'Nothing in particular.' Her gaze returned to the page. 'Except that you've been muttering some slightly odd things in your sleep lately. Just bad dreams, I expect. Or are you subconsciously drafting your memoirs?'

Smiling at the top of her head, Mike bit into the shortcake. He said nothing.

Photoset, printed and bound in Great Britain by
REDWOOD BURN LIMITED, Trowbridge, Wiltshire